FORBIDDEN HEART

"This is all your fault, you know," Mallory said.

Ellis grinned. The time alone had done its magic. The Mallory he loved was back. The grin fell off of his face.

Loved? Mallory Heart? They hadn't known each other long enough for him to love her.

Ellis stared at Mallory for a long moment.

"What's wrong?" she asked as she rose. "Is mascara running down my face?"

"Huh? Uh, no. No. You look fine. Let's go," he said, taking her hand.

"I'm not the one standing here making demands. I've just lost my license. I can't drive for three months. Do you know what an inconvenience that's going to be?"

But Ellis wasn't really listening to her. He was staring at her mouth.

"What?"

He snaked an arm around her waist and pulled her to him. When his lips covered hers, Mallory's argument and accusations died away. It was as though they were the only two people in the courthouse.

She pressed closer to him, her hand sliding across his crisp white dress shirt. His lips were warm and sweet on hers—delectable, like candy. It was a kiss her tired, abused soul needed for nourishment. She cherished the moment. Her senses reeled as if short-circuited, and Mallory knew that this was meant to be. At this moment. With this man.

Forever.

"Let's go," he said.

This time, Mallory didn't object.

Novels by Felicia Mason

FOR THE LOVE OF YOU
BODY AND SOUL
SEDUCTION
RHAPSODY
FOOLISH HEART
FORBIDDEN HEART

Published by BET/Arabesque books.

FORBIDDEN HEART

Felicia Mason

BET Publications, LLC
www.msbet.com
www.arabesquebooks.com

ARABESQUE BOOKS are published by

BET Publications, LLC
c/o BET BOOKS
One BET Plaza
1900 W Place NE
Washington, D.C. 20018-1211

First Printing: March, 2000

10 9 8 7 6 5 4 3 2
Printed in the United States of America

This book *never* would have been written without the support of and assistance from five extraordinary individuals who endured all of the neurotic moments, fought the battles that needed to be fought, and asked all the right questions:

Tom Coe
Linda Hyatt
Loretta Pridgen
Beth Simko
Karen Thomas

Your prayers and prodding made it happen. I don't have the words to express my gratitude. In lieu of those words: Thank you.

Shout outs also to Laurie Leclair, Lynn Emery Hubbard, and Day T. Smith for reminding me of what matters most.

Chapter 1

Mallory Heart refused to take "no" for an answer.

"I don't think you understand," she told the man on the telephone. "I have a deadline to meet and these diagrams you people sent over are just all wrong. I will not tolerate incompetence."

After a moment, an arched eyebrow rose at the man's reply.

"Put your supervisor on the line this instant."

Mallory's foot tapped a mile a minute on the parquet floor in her condo. She glanced at the slim Swiss watch on her wrist as she impatiently waited to talk to someone with some authority.

She took a deep breath and was about to yell into the receiver when a rich baritone came over the telephone line.

"This is Bailey. What can I do for you, ma'am?"

Mallory shook her hair back, sending her long micro-braids swinging. She had a few choice thoughts about what the man on the phone could do for her, and not a single one of them had anything to do with the boutique she wanted to build from the ground up.

She wondered if the body and the face matched the voice. Probably not. They never did. So, in an instant she was back to business.

"There seems to be a problem. Your company is supposed to be doing construction on my new shop. I'm looking at this work order and it's not at all as I specified."

"What's your name, ma'am?"

"I am Mallory Heart." She said it with authority, with presence, with the security and the power that befitted every Heart.

"What seems to be the problem, Ms. Heart?"

Mallory, though born and raised in Virginia, didn't have a so-called Southern accent. This man did—in spades. The drawl told her he hailed from the Carolinas or maybe Tennessee. While Mallory normally preferred cultured and articulate city-bred men, there was something about this man's voice that told her he'd take care of business.

And right now, taking care of business held top priority. If she could get this contracting company to get its act together, she could get her own business launched.

"Well, the first problem," she said, "is that I was told someone would call before work began. I haven't heard from anyone."

"One moment, please, Ms. Heart," he said.

She heard paper rustling on the other end and assumed he was flipping through a stack of documents on a clipboard.

"Here it is," he said. "We're scheduled to knock down the walls next week—on Tuesday. My crew will be there at six o'clock in the morning. Please make sure someone is available to let them in the building."

"That's the problem," Mallory said. "The first of several," she added, just barely under her breath. "I have a contract right here that says you're supposed to start tomorrow. When I didn't hear from you people, I called to find out what time I should be on the site tomorrow."

"Hold, please," Bailey said.

Before she had a chance to protest, dead air hummed on the line. Mallory harrumphed. She hated being put on hold almost as much as she hated dealing with incompetent people.

She snatched up her coffee mug. Half of the lukewarm liquid splashed on her hand and the counter top.

Mallory swore, the word rolling off her lips before she remembered she was trying to cut back on that.

"Consuela!" She called for her housekeeper, the irritation she felt coming out in a yell that pronounced every syllable in the woman's name.

"Just a minute, Miss Mallory," Consuela answered, from some distant corner of the house.

"What is this, put-Mallory-on-hold day?" Mallory mumbled.

"Ms. Heart?"

"Yes," she snapped into the telephone receiver, as she dumped the remaining coffee in the sink.

"There seems to be an error."

"That's what I've been trying to tell you." The saccharine sweetness in her voice could in no way be mistaken for friendliness.

"I've double-checked all of our paperwork," Bailey said. "According to our documents, we're not scheduled to be on your site until Tuesday, July eighteenth."

Sexy voice or not, Mallory was beginning to lose what little patience she had left with the man. "And I'm telling you, you're supposed to be here tomorrow. Tomorrow is July eleventh. I have it right here in black and white. I've rearranged my plans so I can be there."

"I'm sorry, Ms. Heart . . ."

She cut him off before he could finish. "Who

exactly is in charge at Quality Construction? I want to speak to the person in charge."

"Ms. Heart, I'm sure there's an explanation. I'll send someone out to see what's what. Where can you be reached in about thirty minutes?"

"I'll be at the shop. You know," she added, "the place you all are supposed to be tomorrow."

"Ma'am, I'll have someone meet you there in half an hour. Please bring all of your paperwork."

"Don't worry," Mallory snapped. She slammed the telephone down before anything else could be said on either end.

"Miss Mallory, you called for me?"

With one hand on her hip and one braced on the cherry-colored counter, Mallory stared at a point beyond Consuela's shoulders. "You know, good help is just hard to find these days."

"You mean me, Miss Mallory?"

Mallory's gaze focused on the crestfallen face of the woman who had been keeping her house clean for the last two years. "No, not you, Consuela. You're a gem. It's those idiot contractors."

Mallory paced the gallery trying to work off the nervous energy that raced through her. Her lifelong dream—well, her amended lifelong dream—was so close. In just a few short months she would be able to shove her success in the faces of all the people who'd gleefully stabbed her in the back.

So close. And yet so very far away.

A million details had to be seen to before she tasted the sweet nectar of victory—and got to say "up yours" to that no good, lying . . .

"Miss Mallory, you worry yourself too much," Consuela said, as she reached for a paper towel and wiped up the spilled coffee. "If you are not careful, you will be like your cousin, Mister Cole. You know, he drinks Mylanta for breakfast."

That got a chuckle out of Mallory. "Serves him right, the way he's treated me."

Consuela shook her head, worry etched on her brow. "It is not healthy for family members to argue the way you and Mister Cole carry on."

That bit of commentary earned a scowl from Mallory. "You don't know the half of it, Consuela."

With an indignant huff, the housekeeper turned on the younger woman. "I work for your Mama and for your Auntie Virginia a long time, a very long time. I know all of it. You, Miss Mallory, are the one who needs to learn about family."

Mallory backed down, as she always did when faced with a tongue-lashing from Consuela Lopez. Consuela was the heart-felt mother Mallory never had. Her own mother spent more time chasing dreams and striving than she did raising her daughter. The only love Mallory had ever known, first as a young girl and then as a confused teenager, came from Consuela, not from Justine Heart. Justine wouldn't deign to get jam on one of her suits or tear stains on a silk blouse.

Hugs and kisses and cookies warm from the oven came from Consuela's heart and kitchen. When Mallory had been lonely or frightened or worried, it was Consuela that she went to, not Justine Heart.

"Yes, ma'am," Mallory said.

Placated by the apologetic tone of the younger woman's voice, Consuela smiled. She patted Mallory's hand then hustled to the refrigerator, where she pulled out two bottles of Evian.

"Here, Miss Mallory, do not forget your water. You must hurry, too. You'll be late for work."

That brought Mallory right back to the crux of her problem.

"Hrrmmph," she grunted.

"What is it?" Consuela asked.

"Those trifling men at Quality Construction have the days all mixed up. I'm never going to make the grand opening if they don't get on the ball."

Consuela gathered the papers Mallory had pulled from her soft leather bag. She tucked them into the briefcase, then put the second bottle of water in a carrier and slipped it in the bag. As was her custom, Mallory would drink the first bottle before she got to work.

"Do not worry, Miss Mallory. They come very highly recommended. You know, Quality Construction Company built the addition on my cousin's house. It is beautiful. Everything will work out as it should. You will see. Now go. I have my own work to do here."

Mallory allowed the woman to shoo her out the door. As she slipped into her Mercedes-Benz coupe, Mallory thought about her relationship with Consuela. Long ago she'd given up on trying to break the woman out of the habit of calling her *Miss* Mallory. If anything, Mallory should have been calling the older woman Miss Consuela. But in deference to what she called "her station", and given her longevity with the Hearts, Consuela insisted on "showing proper respect" to all of the Heart family members.

"Including the ones who don't deserve it," Mallory mumbled, as she shifted the car into gear and made her way to the shop that would soon be her ticket to independence and success—without the interfering assistance or aggravation of her so-called family.

The last thing Ellis Carson needed was a know-it-all telling him how to run his business. Bailey, his right-hand man and site supervisor, had already warned him that this Mallory Heart was a demanding piece of work.

Ellis wasn't in the mood for it today. Not that he ever found himself in the mood to deal with the silver-spoon crowd. He glanced at the day planner open on the pickup's seat. He had another appointment in less than an hour. When that one ended, he could finally get to the real business of the day: finishing up the bid on the fitness center project. The deadline was in two days. And he wanted his proposal completely polished before submitting it. The faster he got that one out of the way, the sooner he could get to work on the project bid that would take his company into the big time.

Ellis wanted that fitness center project so badly he could taste it. Winning it would not only put him in the big league, it would make him solvent. Solvency was important to Ellis, even more important than fulfilling his grandmother's only request of him.

Once already he'd had to dip into his own money to make his payroll. He'd built a comfortable nest egg and was more than willing to use it again to make sure his people got paid. But, that just wasn't the way a business was supposed to be run.

"If that check would ever get here," he mumbled. A pretty big client claimed the state had lost the paperwork authorizing a sizable check being cut to them. That, in turn, meant the client had yet to pay Quality Construction. And it was already almost eight weeks into the billing cycle. The "any day now" tune from the client had gotten pretty old. Things were going to get tight for Ellis if that money didn't show up soon.

"Any day better get here soon," he mumbled to himself.

The shrill of the cell phone interrupted his thoughts. Ellis punched the speaker button. "Carson Quality Contracting." Slowly but surely, Ellis wanted to phase in the new name of the construction company.

"What's up, man?"

"Hey," he greeted Bailey. "I'm headed to this job site. I should be there in about," he glanced at his watch, a waterproof Timex, "ten minutes."

"Just thought I'd let you know about the client," Bailey said.

"From your description, she sounds like a joy to work with."

Bailey chuckled. "Yeah, well, whatever. Her name is Heart. As in *the* Hearts."

Ellis frowned. "I kind of gathered that. What are they doing working with an independent?"

"This one struck out on her own. Apparently she's trying to make a go of it, minus the trust fund and the family's deep pockets. I gather this is her first project."

"Rich girl, huh? She'll probably be bored with it before we get the job done. What is it again—knock down some walls, build some others, right? Shouldn't be that difficult once we get this start date taken care of," Ellis surmised.

"Sorry to be the bearer of bad news, my brother."

Ellis made a left turn onto Virginia Beach Boulevard. "I really hate it when you say that. What is it?"

"She eats contractors for breakfast. I hear we're her third."

Ellis swore. He absolutely had to be on time to his

next appointment, the one that finalized a deal to renovate an apartment complex. The project, while small, could pay off in contacts—and contracts—with the management company, which held quite a few larger properties.

"Well, I guess I'll just have to make her happy so we can get on with it. Why'd you take this job anyway, particularly if you know there's some bad history?"

"We need the money," Bailey said.

"Ain't that the truth. I'm there. Gotta go."

Ellis disengaged the phone and pulled into the parking lot of the upscale strip mall. The address alone let him know the sort of clientele this Mallory Heart expected to cater to.

The rich kind.

Virginia Beach had all kinds, from beach bums who made a living harassing tourists to multimillionaires who lived in mansions tucked away behind the trees. The Heart family, of Heart Department Stores, fell into the latter category. Their money was old, the kind of old that had dust on it.

Ellis checked his day book for the exact location of the shop. Confirming the address with his notes, he spied a white two-seater Mercedes convertible illegally parked at the curb in front of one of the shops. A leggy woman in a red suit at the front door of the storefront was the first hint of trouble. He definitely didn't have time for distractions of *that* nature.

But a look-see couldn't hurt.

A slow cruise by the storefronts gave him a nice look at those legs. Good God almighty! They went on forever.

"God bless the fashion designer who brought back the mini skirt."

Ellis Carson had always been a leg man.

With any kind of luck, that woman wasn't the one who'd given Bailey so much attitude. He found a spot in the lot adjacent to the shopping center. With his day planner and a clipboard under his arm, he approached the woman.

"Excuse me, ma'am," he said.

She pushed the door open as she turned toward him.

What a knockout! Her skin reminded him of pecans ripe for the picking. Her eyes were wide, intelligent. She had enough makeup on to accentuate her high cheekbones, but not so much that she looked made up. He liked the long, sassy braids, too. It took every cell in Ellis's body to keep his mouth shut and his eyes locked on her face and away from those legs.

Surely this beauty wasn't one of those beastly and snobbish Hearts.

"Yes?" she said, irritation dripping from her voice.

That brought him up short and his whole perspective changed. That one word had so much attitude in it that Ellis knew he'd found his client. "I'm looking for Mallory Heart."

She glanced down at him, at the well-worn jeans

he'd donned. Her gaze took in the scuffed work boots and made its way back up his body, where it paused for a moment on the black T-shirt with the Quality Construction logo on the breast pocket. Then she gave a sort of—sniff. Just as if he were a side of beef—with a flaw—she'd sized him up and dismissed him.

Ellis wanted to walk away. He didn't need this kind of aggravation. He'd pay his people out of his own pocket first. He wanted to snap at her to lose the attitude, but decided that too many people depended on him. The only motion that gave away his personal thoughts was a thinning of his lips.

"You're Bailey? Come on. As I said on the telephone, your people are supposed to be here tomorrow, not next week."

She marched ahead of him and kept right on going. Ellis didn't follow.

People who had no manners had to learn the hard way that Ellis Carson demanded and received respect. She kept rattling off a list of complaints as she walked deeper into the dark recess of the building. About a minute later, when she apparently paused to take a breath, she realized that he wasn't following behind like a pet dog.

"Mr. Bailey, what are you doing standing out there?"

Ellis held his ground even as he felt his blood pressure and his temper rise. Why were the beautiful ones always such bi—

He shut the thought down before he could finish

it. Counting to ten, Ellis took a deep breath to still the anger that roiled inside. And he waited.

A moment later, the woman popped back outside.

"Well?" she demanded.

"Good morning. My name is Ellis Carson. Are you Miss Mallory Heart?"

She glared at him. Then she folded her arms across her chest.

The showdown was on.

They stared at each other, neither willing to give an inch in the battle, both warriors used to playing for keeps. As the moments ticked by, Ellis watched . . . and waited.

In her high heels—totally inappropriate for a construction site, he noted—she stood just a hair shorter than his six-foot frame. This Amazon goddess liked intimidating people. He knew that just like he knew his name.

The problem was, Ellis Carson didn't play games—intimidation ones or otherwise.

After a moment, she smiled. Then she stuck out her hand.

"I'm Mallory Heart. Won't you come in?"

Triumphant, Ellis smiled. He'd won this first battle, but something told him lots more were destined to follow.

Chapter 2

Mallory willed her heart to stop beating a mile a minute. Everything about this man was hard, from the body that made her hot to the eyes that stared at her without blinking.

In the space of a few moments, Mallory felt herself shift from savvy career woman to one-hundred-percent pure, natural woman. She forgot everything that mattered and wondered how she could get to know more about this strong black man who didn't back down.

He was dressed like a steelworker or a ranch hand. Well-worn jeans fit him like a second skin and a black T-shirt hugged his pecs. Later in the day, that T-shirt would probably bear sweat stains earned while laboring in the hot sun that beat down on Virginia in July. He was a black Marlboro man come to life, and Mallory wanted a taste of the forbidden.

The Mallory Heart who subscribed to Millionaire magazine, the Mallory Heart who dated senators and CEOs, the Mallory Heart who'd been to prep school and finishing school and had been voted most likely to own a Fortune 500 company, decided she wanted him.

"Well," she said, the single word clearing her throat if not her thoughts.

He tucked the day planner under his arm. Mallory gave him points for carrying a name brand, the same brand she used, as a matter of fact. She smiled as he flipped through the papers on the clipboard.

"Bailey told me there was a problem. May I see your contractual agreement?"

Mallory blinked. His voice sounded colder than the Arctic in the middle of a blizzard. And if she wasn't mistaken—which, of course, she wasn't—she also detected a hostile tone. What in the world could have caused that? They hadn't exactly hit it off at the door, but that was no reason for brutishness.

In a blink, Mallory returned to the woman she knew well. She straightened her back, held her head high, and looked down her nose at him.

"The customer is always right," she said.

Slowly, he looked up from the papers he was scanning. Then he raised an eyebrow. "Thatta fact, Ms. Heart?"

Mallory folded her arms. "I have deadlines to meet. The grand opening is less than two months away. I'll have stock arriving soon, and this place," she waved a hand at the maze-like cubicles scattered throughout the big room, "has got to get done."

"Your contract, please."

She wanted to slap it into his hands, but thought better of that idea. This man's crew would be responsible for creating the look she wanted her boutique to bear. A contractor with a grudge could lead to all sorts of nasty little delays and problems. One sobering thought about the inspections she'd have to pass and what this rude man could do set Mallory straight.

With a regalness hard won given her state of mind, she handed him the contracts with ease.

He accepted the papers but kept a keen gaze on the viper-tongued woman. Second thoughts about just how badly his company needed the odd small jobs to see them through whispered through Ellis's mind.

"We agreed on . . ."

The pager at his waist beeped. "Excuse me a moment, Miss Heart," he said. Ellis glanced at the alpha-numeric message on his pager and winced. He needed to answer the page as soon as possible, but first, this.

Pressing a button on the small device, he turned his attention back to Mallory Heart.

"I'm not sure where the disconnect happened. Your documents say tomorrow. Ours say next week." He opened his planner, pulled out a gatefold sheet of paper, the large accordion-style pages unfolding so he could study the grid. "I don't have a crew available tomorrow morning. The soonest I can get one here is Thursday."

Mallory frowned.

"I know that's not what you had in mind, but it's the best I can offer given the circumstances. And tell you what," he added. "To make up the time and if it's all right with you, I'll have them work Saturday and Sunday to compensate for the two days lost."

He watched her fold her arms and consider the compromise. "There's an extra charge for weekend work."

For somebody who had beaucoup money, she sure was a tightwad. Maybe that's how the silver-spoon crowd got and stayed rich. Whatever. Ellis wasn't in too much mind to keep standing around, particularly not when he had important people depending on him.

"Not in this case. That's just for this weekend that the crew will work those days. After that, if you require any time beyond the five-day workweek, it's double overtime that will be charged to you."

"Fine."

Mallory stuck out her hand to shake on the deal. For a moment, Ellis stared at her extended hand. It had that soft look. A moment later, his assessment proved correct. This woman didn't do dishes or any other kind of housework—not with hands as soft as hers. She had long, graceful fingers. Her handshake was firm, like a man's. Ellis gave her points for having guts—probably because she gobbled down contractors for breakfast, as Bailey had said.

In another five minutes, he was out the door. Mallory Heart wanted to give him directions on what she envisioned for the shop. After assuring the woman that her eight-page memo and twenty-five-page diagram was sufficient, Ellis high-tailed it away from there. Too much time had already passed since he'd gotten that page. He needed to return the call.

He also needed to get away from those long legs and smoky eyes.

Mallory watched him leave. She didn't follow, although she found herself tempted to do just that. Ellis Carson was rude and domineering . . . and downright sexy in a rough and tumble sort of way. He had the hard-core look that at once appealed and repelled.

Mallory didn't at all like her physical response to him. So she decided to just chalk it up to excitement about finally getting a step closer to realizing her dream. She had to admit, though, the man had to be the best looking contractor she'd ever seen.

Slowly, she walked around the place that would be hers to showcase her talents. She paused here and there, imagining what each spot would look like on opening day. Before long, Ellis Carson had been relegated to a shadow of a memory.

Mallory's Place.

A big grin filled her face. The eponymous name for the shop may have been an ego-booster for her, but she'd needed it, just like she'd need the influential clients she expected to draw from the surrounding area. Mallory's Place gave her the stroking she desperately needed right now.

Ever since she'd been unceremoniously booted from the company she'd given her blood, sweat, and tears for, Mallory had one goal: revenge. She didn't want to get back, she wanted to get even. She would prove them all wrong, particularly her stuck-up, stuffed-shirt cousin Coleman Heart and that witch of a mother of his.

Mallory's stomach tightened and her head started to throb at the very thought of her cousin and aunt. Aunt Virginia's support in the effort to lure the department store chain Knight & Kraus to Hampton Roads had been one big sham, all perpetrated for the sole purpose of humiliating Mallory. Cole had to have been in on it. He had to. He'd been too smug, too nonplussed when his precious little stores were sold right under his feet.

Cole had gambled on the family members seeing things his way. He'd gambled and lost, though. Mallory smiled. Cole's strategic failure had been in underestimating her. So he'd lost in a major way.

Mallory's smile faded as the rest of the story played out in her mind. In the end though, she'd lost too when the Knight & Kraus operations vice president informed her that her services wouldn't be needed beyond the transition period.

She'd believed in the oral agreement they'd made, all the while knowing that if something happened, they could claim it had never existed. The "four corners" of a piece of paper were all that really mattered.

Remembering the conversation made steam practically billow from Mallory's ears. She'd labored to make the deal happen. She'd called in favors and taken giant leaps of faith to broker the deal. Unfortunately, not only had there not been a net to catch her, the ground below was solid concrete.

"Down but not out," Mallory said, as she walked the length and breadth of her new place. "Down but not out." That solace had been her mantra.

With the right financing, the right connections, the right attitude, and the right people around her, Mallory knew that the best way to get even would be to steal their clientele right from under all of their noses.

She walked to the area of the room that would house the complimentary cafe. Free espresso and biscotti would make her customers linger for a while. The more they lingered, the more they'd buy, particularly with shop models walking by in the outfits that could be purchased at Mallory's Place.

"Cole thinks he knows something about customer service," Mallory muttered. "I'll show him what customer service is all about."

Cole's bumbling and fumbling mismanagement had led to the downfall and eventual demise of the Heart stores. Lackluster sales sealed their fate. A moment later, Mallory shook her head. That wasn't true and she knew it. Her cousin Coleman hadn't been at the helm of the company long enough for it to decline the way it had. Years of neglect, mismanagement, and theft by their fathers and uncles had seen to that.

Mallory was, however, confident that she would have been able to turn things around. "I should have been CEO—not that blasted Cole!" she told the empty space of the store.

Cole wasn't even the direct heir to the chairmanship.

That thought brought her pacing to an abrupt halt and shifted her thoughts in another direction. A quiet trip to the country would go a long way toward soothing her rattled nerves.

* * *

"What took you so long?" Bailey asked, when Ellis stomped into the trailer.

"Jeanette paged me. She thought one of the kids was running a fever."

Bailey looked up from the work schedule he plotted. "Ray-Ray?"

Carson shook his head. "Not this time. He's hanging in there. It was Quandra. Jeanette thought it might be chicken pox or something."

"Didn't she already have the chicken pox?"

"Yep." Ellis grinned.

Bailey chuckled. "That Jeanette. She's something all right. You gotta give the woman points for persistence."

Ellis smiled as he pulled off the T shirt that carried a funky mix of sweat and dust. "I'm gonna wash up a bit. It's hot as you know what out there." He headed to the little bathroom in the trailer they used as an office during the busy construction season.

"Why do you think I've been directing things from in here most of the day?"

"Don't you go slacking on me, man. Besides," Ellis said, as water started running, "we've got a commitment for this Saturday and Sunday."

"What do you mean 'we'? I've been trying to hook up with Rhonda for the last three weeks. The woman's gonna think I'm not interested if I put her off again."

"Not likely. She worships the ground you walk on."

"Yeah, like Jeanette does you."

Ellis popped his towel-covered head out of the bathroom. "Hey, now. Don't start that again."

"What's up this weekend?"

This time, instead of a grin, Ellis grunted as he returned to the sink. "That Mallory Heart of yours. By the way, ask Sheila to recheck her data entry. We had one date on the contract and that Heart woman had another."

Bailey jotted a note on a legal pad for their office assistant. "What's that got to do with the weekend?"

"I had to come up with a compromise. I told her we'd get a crew out there Thursday."

Bailey glanced at the week's work schedule attached to the wall. "Green team can go." Quality Construction had four work crews that rotated jobs: red, blue, green, and gold. They were distinguished by their individual specialties and by the color-coded T-shirts they wore to work. "Ned'll be back from vacation tomorrow."

"Make sure you give him a heads-up about that Heart woman. She's a piece of work, all right."

Ellis came out of the bathroom shaking a can of aerosol deodorant. He sprayed under his arms and reached in a locker for a clean T-shirt.

"Uh huh. And what aren't you telling me about this weekend?"

Pulling the white athletic shirt over his head, Ellis

broke the bad news. "I told her we'd work this weekend to make up the so-called lost time."

Bailey shook his head. "Man, that's gonna be expensive. Six guys on double OT. We're barely making . . ."

Ellis held up a hand to halt the too familiar words from his right-hand man. "Two guys. Working for free."

Bailey's brow furrowed. "Where are you gonna get . . ." Then it dawned on him. "Ah, man."

"We've done it before, Bailey-boy."

"Yeah, when we were ten years younger. Do you know how much work you're talking about just the two of us trying to do?"

"Yep. But I'll be damned if that Heart woman is gonna give me any more heartburn."

Chapter 3

Three days later, Mallory arrived at the shop about half an hour before the crew did. She'd made a stop at Krispy Kreme for two dozen assorted doughnuts and lots of coffee. If she knew just one thing about business it was that happy workers were productive workers.

She set the doughnuts and coffee on a table, then called her caterer to confirm the lunch order. Breakfast and lunch weren't included in the contract she had with the contracting company, but good will could be bought. That lesson she'd learned well from her uncles.

After making sure a keg of ice water was readily available in case the construction workers got thirsty throughout the day, Mallory went to the room that would be her office to do some paperwork while she waited.

Ellis woke up on the wrong side of the bed. The digital clock across the room flashed 7:20. A cuss word rolled off his lips as he tossed the cotton sheet aside and, naked, dashed to the shower. Quandra had been running a fever last night. He'd ended up hanging out at Jeanette's much longer than he'd anticipated. The ribs and coleslaw she had waiting for him didn't make leaving any easier. Now he found himself paying for that dalliance.

By the time he got from his house in Newport News to the Virginia Beach shopping center where Mallory Heart's store was located, it was close to nine. A backup in the Hampton Roads Bridge-Tunnel could always be counted on when a man was in a hurry.

Ellis's plan had been to arrive before the crew so he could prep Ned about Mallory Heart. When he walked in the place, though, all of his men were standing around chomping on doughnuts as if he paid them by how much break time they used up in a day.

"What's going on?"

Heads looked up and over his way.

"Hey, Carson. Miss Heart was just telling us about her vision for her store," the crew chief said.

The men parted as though a modern-day Moses issued the command. They rippled back until the only space separating him from her was a sea of black and tan work boots and white powdered sugar on the floor.

Ellis's brow furrowed. They were supposed to be knocking down walls and creating a retail space to spec not standing around discussing "vision."

"Ms. Heart, may I see you?"

His tone told everyone in the room that the question wasn't really a request. A couple of the men eyed each other with "uh oh" looks.

"One moment," she said, barely giving him a glance. She turned to the men. "And so, as I was saying, you are here, creating the foundation for what I hope will be one of the finest establishments in Hampton Roads. When I open, I'll have a discount offer just for you—or your wives or girlfriends," she added, with a smile.

Ellis looked around at his men. They drank coffee, chewed doughnuts, and stared at her like she was a freaking goddess or something. Ellis had to give her points though; she seemed to know the art of sucking up and making nice. But he also knew that few, if any, of his manual laborers would be able to afford as much as a hair pin in the woman's shop, not if her prices were in line with the neighboring businesses'.

The lime-green mini-skirt suit and matching shoes she wore probably cost more than all of his guys would earn in a month.

"I know you need to get back to work," she said. "I just wanted to take a moment to thank you. And don't forget, Maxine's Grille will bring lunch in for you all. I told them to come at about twelve o'clock. Is that all right?" She directed the question to Ned.

"That'll be just fine, Miss Heart. You didn't have to do that. Most guys just bring a bag."

"Well, not today," Mallory said, a sweet smile curving her lips.

Ellis didn't buy the act for half a second. He'd already gotten a taste of how demanding she could be.

"All right," he said, breaking up the love fest. "Let's get back to work. The sooner we get everything Ms. Heart wants done, the faster she'll be able to open her store."

And the faster I will be able to get away from her, he added to himself. For some reason, she'd crawled up under his skin. A glance at her legs, covered in sheer, light-colored hosiery, gave him a good idea of why she distracted him—and annoyed the heck out of him.

It had been a while—a long while—since he'd been with a woman. Jeanette wanted to, all right. But Ellis knew that would be too dangerous. A couple of other women, namely the one at his grandmama's church, had made it clear that they were available.

The problem was, Ellis didn't have time for all of that "getting to know you" business that precipitated every new relationship. All he needed from time to time was somebody to warm the sheets. And of late, he'd been so tied up with getting his company into the next level of contracting, that the last thing he even had time for was a little sumthin' sumthin'.

Mallory Heart, unfortunately, reminded him just how long he'd been without, and just how bad the itch could get. That knowledge, coupled with the bitter irony that it was a rich girl his body noticed, did nothing for the already foul mood he was in.

Ellis folded his arms and watched Mallory work the room of rough-edged laborers. She shook each man's hand as he finished eating. What did she think she was doing, running for mayor or something? Shaking his head in disgust, he impatiently waited for her to finish the pep rally.

A moment later, she ran out of men to charm and stood in front of him. She folded her arms and stared into his eyes. Ellis recognized the smug challenge.

"You wanted to see me?"

Not really, he wanted to say, but instead he heard the words, "I stopped by to see if things were progressing smoothly," came from his mouth.

"Why yes. They were. Until you arrived."

Ellis's eyes narrowed.

"I think we can work this out, Ms. Heart," Bailey called out, as he strode from a room beyond the main floor, studying a piece of paper as he walked.

"Oh, morning, Ellis," Bailey said, when he spied his friend. "I didn't know you were here."

"Thought I'd check on things."

"What do you think?" Mallory asked Bailey. He placed the diagram on a counter top.

"If we move this and construct a platform here, I think you'll get the effect you want."

She smiled at Bailey.

An irrational stab of envy sliced through Ellis. He decided to ignore it.

"Excellent. Let's do it then," Mallory said.

"Do what?" Ellis asked.

"I suggested a few changes," she said. "Bailey agrees and will see to it that they happen."

Ellis raised an eyebrow then glared at his right-hand man. "As you know, we want to stay within the budget and the time frame."

"Not to worry, Mr. Carson. Bailey said his company's weekend crew will have no problem getting things caught up—even with the changes. And do remember," she added, "I'm paying the bills."

With a sudden flash of insight, Ellis realized why she grated on his nerves so much. He held to old-fashioned mores and values. Women were supposed to support men, not compete with them. He had no problem with women who worked because they needed to take care of their families—usually because they'd hooked up with a trifling man who didn't know what it meant to be a man.

Women like Mallory Heart, though, were women who needed a man to remind them that they were supposed to be help mates, not crusaders. In Carson's book, a man took care of his woman and his family and the woman took care of the man. That's the way it was supposed to be.

"You're paying the bills, Ms. Heart. But we're to see that the job gets done to code and to spec. After all, you do want to open on time, don't you?"

Mallory stared at him for a moment, then, disregarding him as though he weren't even there, she turned to Bailey.

"I'd prefer if you keep Mr. Carson out of my store," she said. "I have not liked his attitude from the moment he walked in here Monday. Dismiss him. I don't want him in here."

"Uh," Bailey started, with a pleading look in Carson's direction. "I beg your pardon, ma'am."

Ellis grinned. "Seems like the lady wants me gone, boss man. I'm outta here."

He gave a little bow, turned on his heel, and walked out.

Bailey stood there staring with his mouth open as the man who signed his paycheck stormed out of Mallory's Place. He was going to hear about this, big time. The front door slammed as Carson exited. The workers glanced up, then turned their attention back to their jobs.

Bailey shook his head. "Oh, boy."

"How long have you been in construction?" Mallory asked Bailey. Work for the day completed, the two sat in her office drinking latte that she'd made from the elaborate espresso system she'd had installed.

"Long enough to know that customers don't usually treat the laborers to lunch or latte," he said, holding up his cup. "That was nice of you. The men appreciated it."

Mallory smiled. "Then it was worth it."

She sat back in her chair, fanned herself with a file folder, and unbuttoned the top two shell buttons on her suit jacket. She wore nothing underneath and wondered if Bailey had noticed.

He cleared his throat and sat up.

"Well, I'd better be going. We have a long day tomorrow."

Mallory leaned forward, giving him ample opportunity to windowshop.

"Will you be here?"

Bailey rose. "Ned, the crew chief will be in charge. I'll just pop in to check on their progress."

Mallory nodded and stood up. Bailey took a step back.

"Do I make you nervous, Bailey?"

He stepped back again. "I wouldn't say nervous, Ms. Heart . . ."

"Call me Mallory."

"Ms. Heart," he said, standing his ground, "I think we need to get something clear."

"What is it?" she said.

"I'm in a committed relationship."

"So am I," she replied.

"You are?" He visibly relaxed. Then he smiled. "Well," he said, sticking a hand out to her, "then we understand each other."

"Perfectly." She sat on the edge of her desk and crossed her legs. Bailey watched the motion, swallowed, and apparently decided to leave while the getting was good.

"Good night, Ms. Heart. I'll see myself out."

He practically ran for the door.

Mallory watched his retreat. Her shoulders slumped. "You're just out of practice," she assured herself.

She bit her lip, instant punishment for the lie. Bailey, who hadn't offered if that was his first or last name, ran as if the hounds of Hades nipped at his ankles. Mallory sighed. So much for thinking she could practice her wiles on him. While attractive in a country-boy-next-door sort of way, Bailey didn't even rate on her scale.

"Now that insufferable coworker of his is another story," she murmured. Not, of course, that she would actually consider . . .

Mallory stopped her train of thought because she knew that, being honest, she was already considering the possibilities Ellis Carson presented.

She leaned back, her hands braced behind her, as she thought about today's encounter with Mr. Carson. He didn't like her. That, she knew with certainty.

Since Mallory was used to being unliked, that part didn't bother her one bit. What riled her was her response to him. Though she knew they mixed like oil and water, she found herself drawn to him. A strength exuded from Ellis Carson, a confidence that she couldn't help admire. It mirrored her own—and that was a dangerous combination.

As she slipped from the desk, Mallory wondered what made him so hard. She knew why *she* didn't give any quarter. She couldn't afford to, had never been allowed to.

"But what happened to you?" she asked the absent Carson.

"If she were a man we'd have had it out right there," Ellis said.

He kicked back on the porch at his house. He'd taken a break from the bid he was putting together when Bailey knocked on the front door. A couple of beers and a bag of pork rinds between them, Ellis and Bailey reviewed the day.

"I didn't know whether to laugh or cry when she

said 'Dismiss him.' You're dismissed, Carson." Bailey laughed at the absurdity of the moment earlier in their day.

Carson frowned. All he said was "Hmm."

"She came on to me, too."

"Get outta here," Carson said. "That ice queen? She wouldn't know what to do with a man if she got one."

"Well, she started by unbuttoning a couple of those fancy buttons on that short green suit of hers. The woman has a pair of legs. Man, she makes me understand why you like a woman's legs and feet."

"I do not have a foot fetish," Carson grumbled, "so don't even go there."

Bailey's chuckle sounded over the pager that went off. "That's me," he said, glancing at the number. "Time to roll."

"That your mom?"

"Yep. I promised her I'd take her to a movie tonight."

"Later, then," Carson said.

Long after Bailey left, Carson turned his friend's words over in his mind. The only thing Mallory Heart could unfasten for him was her checkbook.

Chapter 4

The next day, Carson reviewed the upcoming two months' worth of work, then checked in with his office assistant. He didn't want to be disturbed for anything, and that included calls from Jeanette and her children. While he loved them as if they were his own, he did have a life and a company to run.

He shook his head. "Who knew that adopting a Little Brother would mean taking in the whole family?" He didn't begrudge the time he spent with Antwan and his siblings, he just couldn't be their chauffeur, cook, handyman and babysitter every moment of the day.

After telling Sheila in no uncertain terms that he meant *no* calls, Carson sequestered himself at the conference room table to bone up on everything there was to know about Knight and Kraus.

The mid-Western company had recently announced plans to expand into the Hampton Roads market. They'd bought out the local Heart Department Stores, planned to completely renovate the three existing Heart stores in the area, and then build additional stores from the ground up.

"Too bad the Hearts can't keep their renegade family members in check," he mumbled, as a mental vision of Mallory Heart came to mind. That family sure had a reputation, most of it negative. Carson wondered what it was that made rich black people forget where they came from.

Shaking his head, he focused back on the notebook computer and the papers spread in front of him.

Undoubtedly, the Knight & Kraus project was one of the most ambitious to hit the area since Norfolk's MacArthur Center mall was announced. The chain of department stores planned a presence in every single one of Hampton Roads' malls, as well as the stand-alone locations of the Heart stores.

The thought of winning the contracts to do all that work made him grin. "Money, money, money," he said.

While the bid process was competitive, Carson knew that Quality Construction had an edge—the company specialized in renovation work. While it wasn't as large as some of the other local outfits he expected would have an interest in the project, his company had the nimbleness, the creativity, and the reputation as a solid, honest contracting firm capable of doing big jobs as well as small ones.

Carson had worked long and hard to develop and maintain that reputation. And he was tired of depending on the fickleness of government contracts and the folks who depended on them to get his money to him. Making a few notations on the legal pad next to his laptop, Carson soon found himself immersed in the work.

He started when the telephone rang sometime later. As the line rang a second time and then a third, he finished up the calculation on which he had been working. Leaning back on the hind legs of his straight-backed chair, he snatched the cordless from its home on a low filing cabinet before it kicked over to the answering machine.

"Carson here."

"We've got a problem," Bailey said, without preamble.

Carson sighed. "What?"

"I think you need to come down here."

"Here, where?" Carson asked, even though he had a sinking feeling he knew exactly where here might be. Every job they had going right now rolled along smooth as butter—except for one.

"Mallory Heart's place."

Carson closed his eyes and counted to ten. A moment later, suitably composed, he was ready to deal with whatever presented itself to be the problem.

"You know I'm trying to get a draft of this bid done. You're supposed to handle things, Bailey. What's the deal, man?"

"Sheila told me you told her you weren't to be disturbed."

"Then why am I talking to you, huh?"

"So she's had me paged nine times today," Bailey said. "Ned's called direct another eight."

Carson glanced at his watch. It was barely noon. "So are you gonna tell me what's up or is this supposed to be Twenty Questions?"

"Get down here."

"What the . . . ?"

Bailey cut him off before he could launch into an irritable tirade. "Two guys on the green team have quit and another three, including Ned, are threatening to walk out."

"Oh, man."

Carson slammed the phone down and beat it to his truck. By the time he got to Mallory's Place, he'd decided that the problem with the world today was that women like Mallory Heart were in it.

The first thing he saw were his men standing outside, arms folded, looking highly put out.

"Where are Ned and Bailey?" he asked one of them.

"In there arguing with that cobra," Johnnie answered, as he took a drag on a cigarette. "I shoulda known something was up with her when she came on all nice with the doughnuts and lunch yesterday. That chick is nuts."

Carson glanced around. This wasn't exactly the kind of retail rent district where people loitered outside smoking.

"You all take an hour," he told his employees. "When you get back, I'll either have this straightened out or I'll assign you to another job."

"What about our pay?" Johnnie said.

"You'll get a full day's pay no matter what happens here."

Satisfied with that, the construction crew headed to their trucks and vans on the far side of the parking lot. With the expensive promise to his men already giving him heartburn, Carson stomped into the shop. Raised voices greeted him, and he followed the sound to the office.

"Your people have not been doing anything right!"

Carson rolled his eyes. He knew who *that* was.

"Ma'am, we've been trying to do everything . . ." Ned, the crew chief, started. "It's just not possible, not with . . ." His voice trailed off, the hesitancy in the foreman's voice clearly borne of not willing to offend the client.

"They haven't been able to work, Ms. Heart, because you've been underfoot all day," the normally unflappable Bailey fired back. "They can't do their jobs if you're hovering and changing specs and making a general nuisance of yourself."

"How dare you speak to me that way. Just who do you think you are?"

Carson stepped into the ring. "He's my right-hand man, Ms. Heart. And the reason I'm here is because apparently work around here has been idled. What's the problem?"

Ned gave a visible sigh of relief. "Mr. Carson, I've been trying . . ."

Carson held up a hand to halt Ned. "Just a moment, Ned. I'd like to hear from Ms. Heart."

Mallory stared between Bailey and Carson. "What are *you* doing here?" she demanded of Carson. "I ordered you not to set foot on my property again."

Carson motioned for Ned to leave. With a sigh of relief, the crew chief quickly scuttled out of harm's way and shut the office door on his way out.

"Well, that can, of course, be arranged, Ms. Heart," Carson answered Mallory. "As a matter of fact, it's probably not a bad idea at all. If you'll kindly write out a check for the time we've spent here, plus the wages my men have lost today, we'll consider the contract null and void. You can find another contractor."

"Carson, are you sure?" Bailey asked.

Carson shrugged. "It's not worth the hassle," he said, looking straight at Mallory.

"What authority do you have?" she demanded of him.

Carson tucked his hands in his jeans pockets as he assumed an "ah, shucks" stance. "Well, Ms. Heart, seeing that I own the company, I'd say quite a bit."

Mallory's gaze whipped between the two. "I beg your pardon, but I thought . . ."

"Must have been a first," Carson muttered, under his breath.

Bailey stifled a smile.

"You assumed that because I was the person you were led to initially, that I owned the place," Bailey told her. "Yes, I'm in charge. But Ellis Carson here is the sole proprietor of Carson Quality Contracting."

If a lemon had been in her mouth, Mallory's lips couldn't have been more puckered and put out. She stomped away to her desk, the thick heels of her open-toe shoes leaving an angry tattoo on the bare floor.

"I have a deadline to meet and I expect you all to meet it."

With a deliberate slowness that he knew would be interpreted as intimidating, Carson withdrew his hands from his pockets and advanced on her until he stood directly opposite her, her cluttered desk the only barrier between them. When she didn't back down or even flinch, Carson had to give her mental points for guts. Mallory Heart liked to play hardball.

Well, so did he.

From the corner of his eye, Carson saw Bailey slide into a chair to watch the show. He didn't have long to wait, because Carson had taken just about all he was going to take from this haughty diva.

"I'm going to ask you this just once, Ms. Heart, so listen up well," he said. "Why is it that after a day and a half of working for you, two of my most valued employees up and quit and another three are threatening to do the same thing? They've worked together on quite a few projects and have always done exemplary work. What happened here?"

Mallory glared at him. Something in his eyes taunted her; he'd tossed down the gauntlet and dared her to pick it up. Energized by the tension in the room, Mallory rose to the occasion.

"Your so called 'exemplary' employees couldn't follow even the most basic of directions. I'd say what happened here, *Mr.* Carson, is an outbreak of incompetence."

Carson's eyes narrowed, but he didn't gobble the bait. "In what way?" he calmly asked.

If she'd known him at all, she would have known to tread carefully. But from what he'd already experienced of this woman, Mallory Heart was the proverbial bull in a china shop.

Mallory snatched up a blueprint and pointed to an

area marked with yellow sticky notes. "All they had to do was knock out this wall and replace it there," she said, pointing to a spot barely two feet away. "I mean how complicated can it be? I was led to believe," she said, stressing the words "led to" as she glared at Bailey, "that you people knew how to do at least that basic sort of contracting work."

Carson glanced over his shoulder toward Bailey, who'd leaned back in his chair. " 'You people.' Funny how that sounds coming from our people, huh?"

Bailey just sort of shrugged. He knew just how close to the edge his friend was and wondered if Mallory Heart even suspected.

Turning back to Mallory and her modified diagrams, Carson pointed to the wall shown on the paper. "This is the wall you want torn down?"

"Yes."

He turned toward his friend again. "Bailey, now why didn't you just tell Ned and the crew to follow the lady's directives? This doesn't seem so unreasonable a request."

For the first time, Mallory smiled. Carson watched the tension ebb from her body. Out of nowhere, he wondered what she'd look like completely relaxed, sated from a long, hard night of lovemaking. But before that image could root and spread elsewhere, Carson shut down the train of thought. Sleeping with this woman would probably be like sleeping with a black widow; she'd bite his head off after it was all over.

He'd been momentarily grateful that brown slacks covered her legs today. The very last thing he needed was the distraction of her legs. Then again, her body was slamming. Unfortunately, everything coming out of that mouth ruined it all.

He picked up the diagrams. "Come on out here. Let's see if we can take care of this for you."

Mallory eyed him. "Why are you being so reasonable all of a sudden?"

He smiled, but she noticed little true humor in the gesture. "Like you said the other day, 'the customer is always right.' Right, Ms. Heart?"

Carrying her marked-over diagrams, Carson left the office fully expecting her and Bailey to follow. He stepped around a temporary workhorse and made his way to the wall illustrated on the diagram.

"This is the one you want to get rid of, correct?"

Mallory nodded. "Yes, you see, by moving it here," she said, stepping two footsteps away, "I'll get better light from that window. A half wall, constructed of that see-through glass brick material should replace it. The top part will be covered with plants. It will be very warm and inviting for customers to relax around some natural greenery."

She cocked her head to the side, caught up in her vision and dream for her store. "You know," she said,

"I hadn't considered a fountain, but those are very soothing, too, don't you think?"

Carson stroked his goatee. "I see your point about the wall and the natural light."

She brightened. "Excellent! Well, now that that's all straightened out, there was the matter of the dressing room areas." She started toward where the customer changing rooms would eventually be located. "Your crew chief refused to . . ."

"Ms. Heart," Carson called.

She turned, the hint of a satisfied smile easing away the lines of stress that had been apparent just a few minutes ago.

"And how would you like your roof rebuilt?"

Mallory frowned. "What?"

Carson pointed toward the ceiling. He caught Bailey's eye as the other man looked toward the front door, trying not to crack a smile.

"The roof," Carson clarified. "Did you have a plan for the ceiling and the roof?"

She eyed him from head to toe even as her frown deepened. "Mr. Carson, the roof, as you well know, is going to stay right where it is. It's the interior that's being redone here. It's all plain as day on the diagrams you're holding."

Carson nodded, condescendingly. Then he lost it, slapping the blueprints against the offending wall. "Not, Ms. Heart, after you tear down *this* wall. It's a support wall. But, of course, you already knew that because you know everything there is to know about everything. Right?"

Mallory hustled back toward him and snatched the papers from his hand. "What do you mean, a support wall? This one is a false wall, just like most of the others. That's the one that supports the building," she said, pointing to a wall opposite the one where they stood.

"Oh, really?"

"Yes, really. I know this place like the back of my hand. I know every nook and cranny, every square foot of it."

"That a fact?"

She folded her arms and glared at him. "Yes, that's a fact, Mr. Carson. Now I'd suggest you get your men back in here so this project can conclude on time and within budget."

"Bailey."

In an instant, Bailey stood at Carson's side. "There's a sledge hammer in the back of my truck. Would you go get it, please?"

Within moments, Bailey was back, hauling the heavy tool on his shoulder. Handing it over to Carson, Bailey stepped aside, assuming a position well out of Carson's way.

"What are you going to do with that thing?" Mallory demanded.

Without a word, Carson hefted it. "This is the false wall, right?"

Mallory took a step back. "That's already been established."

"Just wanted to double check your facts," Carson said. "We wouldn't want to make any incompetent mistakes now, would we?"

With that, he slammed the hammer into the wall she'd insisted was the support one. Plaster and paint chips exploded all around them.

"Have you lost your mind?" Mallory shrieked.

But even as she took a breath to let loose a thorough tongue-lashing, she noticed the big, gaping hole in the wall—a false wall she could see straight through to the other side. Not in evidence could she spy any bit of concrete or other material of substance.

"Wait a minute. That's not supposed to be that way." She turned and pointed toward the other wall, the one she'd insisted was a false wall.

A moment later, the ramifications of what she'd been about to order his men to do sank in. "Oh."

She glanced between the two walls and then the two men. "Oh."

Carson practically flung the sledge hammer at Bailey. "Yeah, 'Oh,' Ms. Heart. Now who is the incompetent one? If any one of my crew had been stupid enough to listen to you, half of them would have been dead or injured by now. And you know what, Ms. Heart, you're not worth that kind of sacrifice."

He jerked his head toward Bailey, who hefted the sledge hammer and headed toward the door.

"You want to know why you can't keep a contractor, Ms. Heart?—and yes, I know all about the other ones you ran out of here—It's because you think you know it all and you don't know jack. I'm sending you a bill for wasting my company's time."

Without another word, Carson walked out of the store.

Shell shocked, Mallory stared at that wall. This was supposed to be her place, her pride and joy. Yet, everything from the moment she'd decided to launch out on her own had been a disaster.

For a long time after they'd left, Mallory stood in the middle of the floor. Her dreams lay in ruin. Quality Construction had been her last hope to get everything finished so she could open on time.

She walked to the wall with the hole in the middle of it, the one she'd insisted was a support wall. Putting her hand through the hole, Mallory felt the first tear fall. Before long, a steady stream followed.

Four hours later, Mallory stood on the threshold of Carson Quality Contracting's front door. The business took up a small unit in an industrial park mall in Hampton. A young woman looked up when the door buzzed.

"Hello, I'm Sheila. How may I assist you?"

Mallory clutched her handbag. She'd changed from the summer brown pants-suit to a short but elegant red mini skirt suit. Her crying jag had ended with her on the floor at Mallory's Place, sitting in the middle of sawdust and debris. Eventually, she'd locked up the shop and gone home to nurse her wounds and her pride.

This time, she didn't need Consuela to set her straight. Mallory had learned a lesson today, a painful one that hadn't been on the curriculum at the business school where she'd earned an MBA.

"Mallory Heart to see Mr. Ellis Carson."

The welcoming smile fell off the receptionist's face.

Sheila glanced back at the door behind her. "Uh, I don't think . . ."

"Tell him I've come . . . that I've come to apologize."

Mallory took a deep breath. There. She'd said it. Granted, not to the person who needed to hear it, but at least the words could come out of her mouth.

With a dubious look at the well-dressed woman in front of her, Sheila picked up her telephone receiver and pressed a button.

"Mr. Carson, Ms. Mallory Heart is here to see you."

Sheila flinched and snatched the phone away from her ear. "She's right here, sir. Standing in front of me. No, I'm not joking."

Mallory wanted to squirm, but she held her ground. Carson's opinion of her came through loud and clear on the half of the conversation she was hearing.

A moment later, the door beyond the receptionist

snatched open. Ellis Carson stood there. The first thing Mallory noticed was the deep scowl on his face. The second was that all he wore were jeans and a towel around his neck.

Chapter 5

Desire slammed through her and almost knocked her down. Mallory reached for support from the chair back just to the side of her in the reception area. In all her years, she'd never been so aware of a man and all the ways a woman's body was built to complement a man's. Her mouth, suddenly dry, didn't seem to know how to operate.

With a deep yearning kind of longing, she stared, taking in every nuance, from the tiny scar on his foreshoulder to the way she envied the white towel draped casually over his other shoulder. She wondered if his skin would be warm to the touch.

"I, . . . I . . ."

Mallory clamped her lips shut. Never in her life had she been tongue-tied. But she was finding it difficult to concentrate when faced with that solid wall of brown muscle in front of her. The fact that he infuriated her didn't help ease the attraction one bit.

"Can't you put on some clothes?" she snapped.

He tugged the towel down and wrapped an end of it around his arm. "Lady, if that's your idea of an apology, I suggest you demand a refund from your finishing school."

With that, Carson turned back into the office and slammed the door.

Mallory flinched. Sheila winced.

The two women stared at each other for a moment.

"That's not what I meant to say," Mallory mumbled with a sigh. Then, embarrassed by the weakness her comment may have revealed, she straightened.

"Would you like to see Bailey?" the office assistant offered. "He's not in right now, but I can page him for you."

Mallory took a deep breath and wrapped herself in the detached independent persona she'd spent years perfecting. "No," she said. "No, thank you. It's Mr. Carson I came to speak with."

With that, she marched to the office door, gave one sharp rap on the wood, and walked in.

"Ms. Heart . . . ," Sheila tried to intervene. The office assistant cast a worried glance toward the office.

Carson had been in a foul mood since he'd left this particular client earlier in the day. He and Bailey spent an hour talking about nothing else. Deciding she didn't want to get caught in the inevitable crossfire between Carson and a problem customer, Sheila locked up the files and shut down her computer, then grabbed her purse and hightailed it to safety before World War III started.

"Sheila, is that witch with a B gone yet?" Carson called out, when he heard a door shut.

"No, she's standing right here," Mallory answered.

It took no time at all for his head to pop out of the restroom. Carson paused in the process of pulling on a white T-shirt.

He glared at her. "Oh, pardon me, Ms. Heart. I didn't know it was you. I'll just change into my tux for you."

Since she knew she deserved it, Mallory accepted the sarcasm. Besides, this man and his company were her last opportunity to see her dream come to fruition. If she had to eat a double portion of humble pie, Mallory figured she may as well make it go down easy.

"I'm sorry about what I said," she told him. "That's not what I'd intended to say."

Carson looked at her. "What was it you'd intended to say?"

That you're the sexiest man I've met in a long time. That

I'd like to take a tumble in the sheets with you. That you make me want things that are out of my bounds.

Mallory swallowed, then licked her lips. "That I didn't mean to come off as such a hard case back at the store. I, well, I made a mistake in reading the diagrams."

Carson nodded as he reached for a shirt and pulled it on over the T-shirt. Mallory started to protest. She'd been enjoying the view . . . immensely.

"A mistake that could have cost more than dollars to fix, Ms. Heart."

Mallory's attention wasn't on his words, though. Out of nowhere, a thought occurred to her. He couldn't think any worse of her than he already did. Why not go ahead and throw caution completely to the winds of chance?

"You look great," she said, as he started buttoning the buttons. Actually, he looked much better than great.

Carson paused in mid-button. "Excuse me?"

"I believe in complimenting things I like," she said, meeting his bold stare.

A half-smile, considering and wondering, quirked his mouth. "Well, so do I. And that suit is talking," he said.

He took a step toward her. Mallory stood her ground, but let her gaze leisurely wander over his hard physique. This was a man who kept his physical machine in optimum condition . . . and it showed.

With warmth, her own body responded to the in-kind assessment from him. She watched him size up her figure. A delicious shudder heated her body.

Suddenly, the very air around them seemed charged with waiting and with wanting. And with the knowledge that what flowed between them had its birth in their first confrontation and would see itself to its natural conclusion, no matter what the two participants happened to decide along the way.

He took another step forward. Mallory licked her lips.

His nearness was overpowering. She ached for something she couldn't name.

Her scent made him weak. Carson desperately wanted to know if she'd dabbed a bit of that sensual-smelling earthy perfume between her breasts.

"What do you want, Mallory Heart?" he asked, softly.

Their gazes locked together, Mallory had no choice but to answer. Everything in her being urged her, begged her, cried for her to tell him, to just put all the cards on the table and let the fallout happen the way it would. But even as those words formed in a part of her, the rational and shielding part of Mallory woke up.

"I want you to build my store."

"Hmm," was all he said, considering her for a long moment, which bordered on uncomfortable. "That's funny, because I got the distinct impression you wanted something else."

"You're trying to embarrass me now," she said.

Carson stepped up to her, completely invading her space, giving her nowhere to run, nowhere to turn. "Be careful what you ask for, Ms. Heart. You just might get it."

Before she had time to register a protest, he'd moved away, far away.

"The delays this week have been on your part," he said, from across the room. "I take it you're trying to beat some kind of deadline. Well, let me tell you this. It's not going to happen if you keep interfering."

"I know."

"And my crew has to work from a set of architecturally-approved diagrams. You can't run around moving supporting walls."

"I know."

He looked up from the paper he'd picked up. "Aren't you being uncharacteristically accommodating all of a sudden?"

Mallory took a seat in one of the two available chairs. Crossing her legs, she prepared for the battle, since the skirmish seemed to have been declared a draw.

"You don't know me well enough to know if anything is characteristic of me or not."

Carson lifted an eyebrow even as his gaze dipped to her legs. "Hmmm," was all he'd commit to.

"I didn't come here to argue, Mr. Carson. I came to apologize and to ask you to reconsider your decision to back out of our agreement."

He leaned against the edge of his desk. "So, what is this all about?" he asked, with a general wave in her direction.

Mallory looked over her shoulder and then back at him. "What?"

"You." he said, leaning forward. "Is this supposed to be the sexy sell? 'If he didn't go for the demanding diva role, maybe the sex kitten ploy will get him.' "

Mallory's mouth dropped open. *Sex kitten?* Flattered and insulted at the same time, she could only stare at him. Insulted won the match. A moment later, she rose.

Mallory's Place wasn't worth this sort of aggravation.

"Mr. Carson, we obviously just can't work together. I came here to apologize, but apparently that was also a mistake in judgment." She slipped the strap of her purse over her shoulder and reached for the door knob.

Carson recognized defeat in her and didn't like the look one bit. In one swift move he was at her side. One large hand shut the door she'd opened.

For a moment, they stood next to each other, quiet, her head slightly bowed in front of him.

"You didn't strike me as a quitter," he said.

Mallory's head snapped up.

"Ouch!" he complained, as her head connected with his chin and her braids glided over the skin open at his neck.

"You shouldn't have been so close," she snapped, as she turned to face him.

Behind the hand that rubbed his chin, Carson smiled. The fire that matched her suit was back. Sparring with this woman gave him a rush that he hadn't realized he'd been missing.

She had a mouth and a half on her, but she also had legs that made him like looking at her.

"What are you smiling at?"

Carson shook his head. "You."

"Well, stop it."

That only made him smile even more broadly.

"I amuse you?" she asked.

"No," he replied, as he edged closer to her. Mallory, her back already against the closed door, had nowhere to go. "You make me want things," he said.

Her gaze locked with his. Their breathing deepened.

"Want what?" she said, the words barely a whisper between them.

Carson's eyes darkened, then his head lowered. Mallory lifted a hand, not in protest, but to finally, finally feel the skin of the man. When his mouth closed over hers, she moaned. A dreamy intimacy settled between them.

It was a kiss to heal her tired and abused soul. It was a kiss that breathed new life into him.

Her palm soothed across his chest as his hand entwined in her braids. The embrace said all of the things they couldn't seem to voice: I'm sorry. Let's get to know each other.

Simultaneously, they realized just what they were doing and broke off the embrace.

Carson turned away, giving her some space. Mallory stared at his back and brought a hand to her mouth.

"I . . ."

He held up a hand. "Sorry."

For a moment, they were quiet. Then a decision was made.

"I promise not to . . ."

"We can finish up by . . ."

They stopped talking. "You first," Carson said.

"If you and your crew will get my store together, I promise not to get in the way. I'll have to be there, because I have work to do in the office, but I'll keep the comments and the suggestions to myself."

"Fair enough," Carson said. "We'll work a couple of nights and weekends to get this over with as quickly and efficiently as possible."

Mallory nodded. "Okay."

Carson nodded, too. "Well." He didn't seem to have anything else to add.

Mallory shouldered her bag and opened the door.

"Thank you." She quickly closed the distance between them and offered her hand to shake.

When he heard the outer door close, Carson sat on the edge of the desk staring at the place where he'd kissed Mallory. That had definitely come out of nowhere.

"Well, not exactly nowhere," he conceded to the erection that strained between his legs. "Damn."

It was bad enough she'd come dressed to taunt him, but he'd fallen for the gambit. And instead of being angry about being played, what he wanted was more, a whole lot more. Passion hummed inside of Mallory Heart. He'd recognized it and responded to it. She kissed as if she hadn't had a lot of practice, which just made him want to be her professor.

Agreeing to work with her would probably be a decision he'd live to regret, but it was too late now. They'd shaken on it. Mallory agreed to stop meddling; and he'd promised to get the work done as soon as possible.

Carson willed his body to relax, to get over her. That kiss had been the first and the last. It was also probably as big a mistake as taking her on as a client, but it was done now.

He nodded, as though convincing himself that that searing kiss had been enough. His body wasn't buying that bill of goods, though. With the taste of Mallory on his mouth and the feel of her indelibly marked in his memory, Carson locked the office.

He did have to get himself together quickly. And he hoped her scent didn't linger on him. He'd promised to take Jeanette and the kids to dinner.

"Mallory, I just don't understand why you're bent on launching this place of yours. Why in the world do you want to put yourself through the stress of a start-up, particularly when you can write your own ticket anywhere?"

Mallory struggled to maintain her patience as she helped her mother prepare a light supper.

"It's something I need to do," she answered.

Justine Heart's concern stemmed from the threat to her own financial well-being, not genuine dismay about her daughter's abilities to make a go of the venture. Mallory wanted to call her mother on that very point, but knew the effort to be pointless. They both knew that Mallory would continue to support her mother no matter where her paycheck came from.

"But what about Knight & Kraus?" Justine whined. "Surely you can go back. Tell them you've changed your mind. Mallory, it's a vice presidency for heaven's sake! You're crazy to walk away from that."

With a ferocity that should have warned Justine to stop pushing, Mallory chopped marinated chicken for their Caesar salads. But subtlety had never been one of her mother's strengths. Mallory tried to remember that as she took her frustration out on the grilled chicken.

Whack! *Slice.* Whack! *Slice.* Chop.

"The poultry is already dead," Justine said, dryly. "I know you think I don't know you wished I was on that cutting board."

Whack!

Mallory's motion to slice through the chicken paused in mid-action. Taking a deep breath, she carefully placed the sharp knife down and braced her palms against the counter. "If you know that, why do you keep pushing me?"

Justine wrapped an arm around Mallory's shoulder. "Because you're my daughter. I just want the best for you."

I'm your meal ticket and you just want what's best for you, Mallory thought. Not for the first time, she found herself angry with her father for creating the convoluted arrangement in his estate that left Mallory in charge of his considerable wealth. If her parents' marriage hadn't been such a farce, Justine could have been living her life now like other women her age—enjoying retirement, traveling, doing anything except making her daughter's life hell.

But there was no need for wishful thinking on Mallory's part. Her father, John Heart, was still dead.

Justine was still her mother, and Mallory still resented both facts.

Taking a deep breath, she broached the issue that had stood between them since the buyout.

"Starting my own store has always been a dream of mine, Mom. If you hadn't pushed me into the family business, I would have been out on my own long before now."

"If I hadn't steered you toward your rightful place in the world, that damn Virginia would have snatched up everything that should have belonged to you from the get-go."

Mallory sighed. This day had already been fraught with so much stress, the last thing she needed now was to have her mother get started on all the injustices, real and perceived, that she'd suffered and the battles fought with Aunt Virginia. The long-lived animosity and battles-royale between the two had sent her cousin Cole to his bottle of Mylanta on a regular basis and caused Mallory more than one migraine through the years.

"Mom, it's not about . . ."

Justine cut her off. "You resent your heritage."

Mallory sighed again. "No, I don't resent the Heart heritage," she said. "I resent being used as a pawn, first in the games you and Daddy played with each other and with Aunt Virginia and Uncle Coleman. And now I resent the fact that you seem to believe

I'm going to run off somewhere with all the money and leave you destitute."

Justine's sharp intake of breath told Mallory she'd probably gone too far this time. But it needed saying, and had needed saying for a long time now.

Justine stood straight up, her dark-complected Patrician features on haughty display. "You, Mallory Heart, are an ingrate."

In a swirl of silks, Justine stormed from the kitchen. A few moments later, Mallory heard her front door slam. She picked up the knife, looked at the chicken on the cutting board, and whacked the knife into the piece of defenseless meat.

As she eventually drifted to sleep, a smile curved Mallory's mouth.

By Saturday, everything was right in Mallory's world. Despite the problems of the last few days, she'd bounced back with the enthusiasm her dream needed to propel itself into reality. After an early workout at her gym then a massage from her masseuse, Mallory felt like her old self again.

She pulled on a pair of capri pants and a short-cropped top, then slipped into her favorite pair of low-heeled mules and grabbed her bag. A few hours at Mallory's Place would do her well. She needed to review the inventory selections she'd made and draft a job announcement for the newspapers and business schools at the local colleges. She planned to create internship opportunities for college seniors. The training she'd received while working in the family business had been invaluable and she wanted to share that with future entrepreneurs.

Mallory had been working for about half an hour when a commotion in the front of the shop caught her attention.

"Hello. Who's there?" she called out, as she rose to investigate.

"Oh, man. I told you that white Benz was hers," Bailey complained. "We're never gonna get any work done."

Carson frowned, but decided he wasn't going to let Mallory Heart's presence hinder the work he and Bailey planned to get done today at her shop. Telling himself he was already over whatever physical attraction he'd momentarily felt for her, he didn't let Bailey's concern faze him.

A moment later, Mallory popped out of the area she'd claimed as office space.

"Oh, hello. I didn't think you'd be here this early."

"Same goes here," Bailey said.

Carson just stared. She was beautiful. In the cut-off pants and with her braids pulled back in a ponytail, she looked like a school girl, a virginal maiden straight from a textbook.

Shaking his head to rid the fancy from his brain, Carson scowled at her. She'd already indirectly contributed to a decided lack of focus. Antwan had called him on it too last night while they played a game of one-on-one. The nine-year-old had beaten him hands down. Losing the game hadn't irritated Carson so much as the fact that the time he spent with Jeanette and the kids, Antwan in particular, was supposed to be quality time, uninterrupted by work . . . or stray thoughts of long legs and smoky eyes.

"I won't get in your way," Mallory quickly said. "I'm just doing some paperwork. As a matter of fact, you won't even know I'm here."

With a wave, she disappeared.

Bailey stared at Carson. "Is she on drugs or something?"

Carson chuckled. "Why do you say that?"

"Is that the same woman who was in here two days ago giving grief like it was a gold medal competition?"

Making his way to the area where he planned to work first, Carson just shrugged. "Maybe she had a revelation," he said.

But he knew their agreement was what had changed her tune. He hoped she would stay in the office the entire time, because already he was feeling the physical effects of seeing her. With a swear, Carson got to work, hoping—in vain—that the manual labor would get his mind off carnal pleasure.

Bailey and Carson had been working together for a long time and quickly got into the rhythm of the job. With the goal of getting this project done as soon as possible, they wasted no time, and the first forty-five minutes zipped by.

"Excuse me?"

Bailey groaned. Carson looked up from the measurement he was taking. Had Mallory even bothered to look at him, she would have thought twice about whatever she was about to say.

"Yes?"

Mallory stood above him with a clipboard in hand. "I was just thinking," she said. "I'd like to make that area a little larger. A review of the inventory I've ordered means the space will need to be expanded. Here's what I want you to do."

Bailey exchanged a glance with Carson.

"Ms. Heart."

She turned and headed to an alcove area, the click of her mules echoing on the concrete floor. "This will eventually be an area for spouses or partners to relax. When you do the wiring, include a third outlet. It's not in the specs, but it shouldn't be a problem. It would be better to have the option of getting three separate channels, maybe for ESPN and ESPN2. The extra outlet will give me some flexibility."

Bailey put his tools aside and waited for the show.

"Ms. Heart," Carson said again.

This time she turned toward him, a one-hundred-watt smile on her face. "It's going to be fabulous! I just know it."

Not at all mindful of the two men watching, Mallory made a three-hundred-sixty-degree swirl as she clutched the clipboard to her chest. "All my life I've wanted—no, I've needed—something for me. Just for me. This is it, guys," she said, opening her arms to encompass the area that would eventually be her retail floor.

"Ms. Heart, we had an agreement."

She grinned at Ellis. "Is this how you felt when you opened your construction company, Mr. Carson? As though nothing in the world could stop you or bring you down?"

Carson shook his head as Bailey watched from the

sidelines. In a matter of mere seconds she'd gone from being a pain in the backside to being, well, kind of nice. The verbal lashing about her interfering ways that he'd already had on the tip of his tongue vanished. In the face of such exuberance, how could he scold her.

"Yeah, Ms. Heart. I remember that feeling," he simply said.

She smiled at him. In that moment, Carson recognized in her a kindred spirit. Though they obviously came from two different worlds, his poverty-stricken and hers practically royalty in the state of Virginia, he felt a connection to Mallory Heart, a connection that could, if given the right conditions, go beyond the surface.

He wondered if she'd ever been hurt the way he had, not in a relationship, but by the world. Shaking his head, Carson banished the thought. The silver-spoon crowd always went to bed with full stomachs and with what passed for clear consciences. It was the rest of the world that burned the midnight oil trying to make ends meet or wondered when what the church folks called "joy in the morning" would ever come.

Suddenly not liking the direction of his thoughts or the charitable way he was feeling toward the busybody, Carson cleared his throat.

"Just leave your instructions over there," he heard himself saying. "We'll get to them."

Bailey's eyebrows rose, but he didn't say anything.

After Mallory disappeared back into her office, Bailey approached the topic. "Hmm, looks like somebody got bit. You're falling hard, fast, my man."

"Stifle it, Bailey," Carson growled. His friend knew him well, though. Ellis Carson was about as old-school as they came. Women were supposed to be the gentler sex. They were to be pampered, taken care of, and, when possible, put on a pedestal. Never mind the fact that lots of two-parent families had both partners working. As far as Ellis Carson was concerned, the man was supposed to take care of and provide for the woman. Period.

Mallory Heart didn't seem the type who'd need or appreciate that kind of man. So as he worked the rest of the morning, Carson tried to keep thoughts of her out of his mind. Unfortunately, the taste of her, the smell of her, the look of her in those sexy tight pants kept getting in the way.

By lunchtime, they'd gotten a lot of work done, but Carson was in a bad mood and it was the rich girl's fault.

"You wanna go get something to eat?" Bailey asked.

"Yeah. What do you want?"

"Doesn't matter. Long as it's hot. And you're paying," he added, with a grin.

Carson harrumphed. "I didn't see her running out here with a catered lunch for us."

"Jealous?" Bailey asked.

Carson just cut his eyes at his friend as he spaced out, heel to toe, the area where he worked. "I don't think little Miss Know-It-All realizes how much space she's gonna lose by expanding the dressing room area."

"You're the one who okayed it," Bailey reminded him.

"That was just to get her to shut up," Carson said. "When I go out, I'm gonna check on some prices for the marble she wants over here. I think we can get her a better price for either the same or a better grade."

Bailey nodded.

Measuring the opposite side, Carson counted off his paces.

"Are you sure that's the way that's supposed to be done?" Mallory said, appearing again on the shop floor. "I have a book on general contracting that says it's good practice to exactly measure the distance between two points."

He stopped in his tracks. Bailey wisely and judiciously kept his full attention on the job he was doing.

"Ms. Heart, the reason we're here, meaning the two of us," he said, pointing first to Bailey and then to himself, "is so we can keep this project on schedule. It's going to be impossible to do that with you offering unsolicited advice every twenty minutes."

"It's been much longer than twenty . . ."

He cut her off. "You know what I mean."

She nodded. "Yes. But I just thought . . ."

Interrupting her again, he spoke over her. "No, that's just it. You think too much. Why don't you go do whatever it is you do and let me do what I do best."

"You are working for me," Mallory reminded him.

The whirr of Bailey's electric screwdriver suddenly died away.

"And like I told you the other day, Ms. Heart, we can fix that quick, fast, and in a hurry. Seeing that two other contractors had to pack up for the same reason, I don't think any court in the land would hold us responsible. What do you think?"

He watched her silently fume. One argument after another flitted across her features. When she folded her arms across her chest, Carson knew she'd settled on a comeback. She opened her mouth, but he cut her off at the pass.

"I'm sure that you put a lot of time and a lot of effort into the plan you came up with for this place," he said. "The memos and the diagrams and the project outline you prepared were thorough. Why are you doubting yourself now?"

That got her.

"I am not doubting myself, Mr. Carson."

Bailey grinned. It was on now. Ellis and Mallory, opposites in every way, were definitely two of a kind. They, of course, couldn't see it, but he did. The sparks between them flew hot and fast. And Ellis rarely, if ever, lost his patience or his cool. That the brother had been discombobulated from the beginning said a lot to Bailey. A whole lot.

"Then why are you running out here changing things every twenty minutes?"

"I told you, it's been longer than . . ."

"It could have been twelve hours, okay. Does that make you happy? The point is, you're doubting the very thing that you put your heart and soul into. Doesn't that strike you as being a little unsure of yourself?"

"You have got a lot of nerve, mister!"

Carson nodded. "That's right. That's how I get by in this world." He unbuckled the tool belt at his waist and dropped it over a sawhorse.

"Where are you going? You can't just leave. We're in the middle of something here."

He looked at her and shook his head. Then Carson held an open palm up to Bailey and flashed three fingers. Bailey nodded.

Mallory stared between the two men, but quickly found herself staring at Carson's retreating back. "What is that?" she asked Bailey, mimicking the hand signal Carson had done. "Where is he going?"

"That means he's taking a break," Bailey said.

"A break! He's barely done any work."

"That's not true, ma'am." Bailey pursed his lips and stared at her.

"What?" Mallory asked, when he didn't seem inclined to elaborate on his troubled expression.

"Ms. Heart, may I ask you a question?"

Mallory folded her arms.

"It's of a personal nature," Bailey continued. "And I mean no harm or disrespect, ma'am."

"What is the question?" Mallory snapped, still looking at the door where Carson left.

"Are you always so mean?"

Chapter 7

Mallory opened her mouth to shriek at him, but no harsh words came. She closed her mouth, opened it again, and pointed a finger at Bailey.

He leaned forward a bit toward her. "Is this the first time you've ever been speechless?"

How dare you! formed in her head. What came from her mouth surprised her.

"That's something I would have expected from your partner," she said, quietly.

"As I said, ma'am, no harm or disrespect intended. It just seems that you've been going out of your way to antagonize Ellis. I realize there was a mistake made somewhere in the office about when we'd start work, but . . ." Bailey shrugged.

"No."

"Beg pardon, ma'am?"

Mallory turned and, intently studying the floor, she walked a few feet away from him before turning to face him again. "You asked if I've always been mean. The answer is no. Or at least, I don't think so. It's been so long though, I can't really recall."

Folding her arms, she hugged herself and gave him a small smile.

"It's funny you mention that," she said. "Just the other night I was thinking back on all of the woulda, shoulda, couldas in my life."

"I've done that before," Bailey said. "It's not an easy lesson."

She glanced at him. "No, it's not."

"What happened?"

This time, she stared at him a long time, assessing him, gauging if he would prove to be friend or foe.

"Where are you from? Originally, I mean," she asked him.

For a moment, Bailey looked surprised at the turn in the conversation. Then, with a shrug, "East Tennessee, a little town you've never heard of, that never even made a map and isn't near anything you ever heard of."

Mallory smiled. "I'm from right here. I was born and raised in Hampton Roads. I've been all over the world though, with school and vacations and work." He realized she wasn't boasting, just stating the facts.

As if coming to some conclusion, Mallory slapped her hands against her thighs. "Have you eaten lunch, Bailey?"

He glanced toward the door that Carson exited. "Uh, no, ma'am. Not yet."

She smiled. "Then come with me, Bailey from Tennessee. I'll share mine and tell you about how I came to be such a bitch."

Bailey, about to accept the invitation, choked when he heard her last words. A coughing fit ensued.

Mallory grinned as it subsided. "No need to seem so shocked," she said. "I've been called worse to my face. Come on," she added, with a wave.

With another reluctant glance toward the door, Bailey followed her into the office. In moments, she laid out a sumptuous spread of cold cuts, French bread and cheeses, and fruit.

"Were you planning on company?" Bailey asked, as she pulled two bottles of Evian from the mini refrigerator.

"No, it was a whim."

"Hmmm," was all Bailey committed to.

After eating in silence for several minutes, Mallory drank from her water bottle then folded her hands. "You know, when I first heard your voice on the telephone, I was attracted to it, to you."

Bailey glanced at the door. "Uh huh."

A rueful smile tilted her mouth. "Don't worry, I'm not going to jump your bones."

Bailey's eyes widened at that.

She chuckled at his expression. "I'm telling you this to explain something."

"Okay," he said, the word a drawn-out dubious question.

"You wanted to know why I'm so mean. Well, here's why. All my life, I've dreamed of finding someone who would love me for me," she said.

The enormity of her words dawned on Mallory, and for a moment, she paused, unsure. The confidence she usually wore as easily as her designer clothes faltered for a moment. Then, taking a deep breath, she rallied. All of her life she'd been taught to go for broke, to trust the gut.

Somehow, Mallory knew that she could trust Bailey, even if she didn't know him that well. She knew like she knew her name that she could trust him and confide in him in ways she'd never be able to with a man like his business partner, Ellis Carson.

"When I first heard your voice," she continued, "I thought it might be you."

"Ms. Heart, why are you telling me this? I'm in a relationship. She's a real nice lady, too."

Mallory smiled. "I'm sure she is. And I'm not telling you these things to make you uncomfortable; I'm telling you so that maybe you'll understand a little better. Maybe you'll understand where I'm coming from."

"Okay," he said. "Where are you coming from?"

Mallory looked down at her desk. "From a place where I was raised to believe I was to take my place in the world no matter what the consequences or the little people ruined along the way."

"And that's the problem with people like you," Carson said, from the open doorway. "You consider anyone not as rich as you, one of the so-called 'little people.' " He dumped a greasy bag in Bailey's lap. "Here's your lunch. But it looks like you had a special invitation to le gourmet catering service."

Mallory's shoulders slumped and she shut down. Bailey swore. "It's not like that, man."

"I have two eyes," Carson said. "Sorry to have disturbed your little tête à tête. I'll go curbside and eat my lunch the way the *little people* do." He stomped off.

"Carson . . ."

"Let him go," Mallory said, a world weariness in her voice. "It's just as well he took what I said out of context. It makes him hate me more. Maybe that'll prompt him to get this job done all the faster."

Bailey stood and reached a hand out to comfort her. "He doesn't hate you, Ms. Heart. As a matter of fact, I'm starting to believe there's a whole lot of something else going on with brother Carson. But you just leave him to me. Finish your lunch," he said. "I'll be back in a minute."

Bailey pulled the office door shut as he left. Ellis had been known to be ruthless, even cutthroat when it came time for business. But never, in all the years they'd been friends, had Bailey ever seen Carson blow up the way he did around Mallory Heart. If two lost souls ever needed each other, it was those two. At one time, Bailey had been a Little League coach, so he knew about building coalitions among hostile contender players.

On his way to placate Carson, Bailey decided his mission was to make things happen between Ellis and Mallory. If they clicked, it worked. If they didn't . . . "Well, at least they'll get some sparring practice in."

By the time Bailey came back, with Ellis in tow, Mallory had cleared up the lunch remains and was staring at a laptop computer monitor.

"Hello," she said, looking up from her work.

The scowl on Carson's face seemed somehow familiar to her. She smiled in the face of it.

"I'm going to go finish that counter top," Bailey said. "I'll leave the two of you to talk." He stressed the last word even as he gave Ellis a small shove.

Carson flexed his shoulder at the contact and glared at Bailey who just grinned as he shut the door, closing Mallory and Ellis in the office together.

Carson stood there looking angry and formidable. Mallory smiled a small smile, the gesture more nervous than welcoming. She saved and stored what she was working on, then closed the computer, stood up, and came around the desk to face him.

Leaning against the desk, she braced her arms behind her. She saw him swallow and wondered what was going on in his head. But more than that, she wondered about the man. The heart-to-heart with Bailey had encouraged her. If she could continue opening up to people, no matter how rocky the beginning of the conversation or relationship, the practice would serve her well as she attempted to make friends.

It might be nice to be more than friends with Ellis Carson.

The thought flitted through her head so fast that Mallory blinked. The attraction to him had been practically instantaneous. Her gut had never let her down before. Maybe, there was something worth pursuing here.

"About the other day," she began.

"Which day? The one where you treated me like a lackey or the one where you had my men quitting left and right?"

Mallory was made of tough stuff. Her resolve didn't crumble in the midst of this sarcasm and anger. Why was he so angry? Maybe, she thought, just maybe . . .

"No," she said quietly, as she pushed off the edge of the desk. She took a step toward him. He eyed her but didn't move.

"I was referring to the day in your office. The day you kissed me."

His gaze roved and lazily appraised her. Her body responded to the inspection. Her nipples hardened; her stomach clenched. She knew what those tell-tale signs meant. Right now, she didn't dare give him a similar once-over. That might be too blatant. She wanted to play this moment just right; she wanted to play it the way her heart was guiding her.

Mallory was glad she'd worn the form-fitting Capri pants. And the mules, well, while they were just a comfortable pair of shoes to her, she knew, from her years in retail at the family stores, that men thought the backless shoes were sexy. Did Ellis Carson think *she* was sexy?

She stepped another pace closer to him and licked her lips.

His gaze went to her mouth. And stayed there.

"I was thinking," she said, "I enjoyed it better when we were doing that rather than arguing."

"I'm a man, Mallory."

When she took a final step, she was in his space. "I know that."

"What are you doing?"

"Going way out on a limb, on a hunch, if you will," she said.

"And?"

Mallory smiled. "And I think the reason we don't

get along very well is because we both know we could get along *very* well."

She lifted an arm, slowly, giving him enough time to pull away, to step away, to halt her either physically or verbally. But Ellis did none of those things. His gaze stayed riveted to her mouth, flicking every now and then to her eyes, studying, assessing the moment and the woman.

In the next moment, she was touching him. Beneath the white T-shirt with the Quality Construction logo, Mallory could feel the heat and the strength of him. She felt in herself an opening, an awareness that she'd never experienced before but didn't have the time right now to analyze.

She leaned forward an inch or two, playing fair, giving him warning of her intent . . . her desire. He didn't move. Not one bit.

Mallory tilted her head, still meeting his intent gaze. Then, closer now, her eyes drifted shut and she kissed him.

The moment their lips made contact, his arm snaked around her waist and he pulled her closer, crushing her against him. Mallory moaned, the sound deep and needy.

A sense of urgency drove her. The kiss sent the pit of her stomach into a wild swirl. She reveled in it, rejoiced in it. She felt his hands cup her face and then splay through her braids as he deepened the embrace.

He burned a trail from her mouth to her neck. This is what she really wanted. Mallory cried out.

Ellis instantly stepped back. He held his hands out at his sides. Her breathing came erratically; she could barely keep her eyes open as sensations poured through her, but she had the presence of mind to ask a single question.

"Why'd you stop?"

"I thought you were crying foul."

She opened her eyes. The passion in her own, she saw reflected in his. Reaching for his hand, she tugged him closer. "My cry was about you. You make me want to holler."

He grinned. "Mallory, if you make that much noise on kissing, you must make love in soundproof rooms."

She straightened, licked her lips, and looked at anything and everything in the office except him. "I, uh . . ."

He reached for her hand and tugged her to him. "Don't," he said. "Whatever's going on here, it's about two people, two consenting adults," he added.

Mallory's gaze met his. "I don't usually throw myself at men."

He stared into her eyes. "Yeah, I think I know that."

"What happens now?"

He grinned as he glanced around the office. "Well, I don't see a bed, but this desk . . ."

"I didn't mean *that!*"

He rubbed against her, letting her feel the extent of his desire for her. "Then tell me what you meant."

"I . . ." She licked dry lips.

Before she could get another word out, his mouth covered hers again. Mallory settled into the embrace, this one easy, exploratory. It was as if he knew he had time now, time to linger and to savor. His mouth moved over hers, devouring its softness.

His hand smoothed its way along her side. The touch sent heat billowing through Mallory. His palm settled at the edge of her breast, close enough to tease, far enough away for her to anticipate and to want him . . . to need him . . . to fulfill the promise of that hand's intent.

But he didn't go that next step. With one final nip at her neck, Ellis put some air between their bodies.

"What happens now?" he asked.

She smiled. "This is where I invite you to dinner," she said.

The sexy smile fell from his face. "I can afford to take you to dinner."

Mallory placed a hand on his chest. "I wasn't talking about taking. I meant invite you to dinner at my place."

His eyebrows rose. "You cook?"

She nodded. "So well it'll make you wanna slap your mama."

Carson chuckled at that. "If I ever slapped Big Mama, that would be my last moment on this earth."

"Who is Big Mama?"

"My grandmother. She can burn in a kitchen. You telling me you can do better than her?"

Mallory smiled. "Well, since I've never sat at her table, I don't know. But I can tell you this," she said. "If retail hadn't been my first love, I probably would have had a little restaurant. You know, one of those places where the chef owns the place and comes out to make sure every customer is content."

"Hmm," was all Ellis said.

"Does that mean you'll take me up on the invitation?"

He studied her. "I have a better idea."

"What's that?"

"I'll take you to dinner."

While she wondered why he'd prefer that to a home-cooked meal, Mallory agreed, suddenly glad he'd made the suggestion. She really knew nothing about this man, and here she was about to take him home, to her private sanctuary.

"I like that idea," she said.

"Good." He smoothed a stray braid back from her face and let his hand linger on the softness of her cheek.

"What's this all about, Mallory Heart?"

She glanced down. "I don't know," she honestly answered. "I want to see, though. Don't you?"

"Yeah. I do." He leaned forward. A gentle kiss sealed the vow.

The rest of the afternoon, Mallory's mind relived the velvet touch of his embrace. Things had progressed a little faster and hotter than she would or could have anticipated, but the new Mallory wasn't going to analyze everything to bits. The new Mallory would enjoy the moment, enjoy the man, enjoy life.

Chapter 8

They'd agreed to meet at Topeka's, a steakhouse. Mallory, more determined than ever to make a go of whatever this was with Ellis, didn't even mention that she didn't eat red meat.

Dinner progressed smoothly. They talked about the things people speak about on first dates: the weather, the tourists, movies. By some sort of unspoken yet mutual agreement, their dinner conversation steered a wide berth around talk about Mallory's store or Ellis's construction company.

After their meal, Mallory suggested drinks at a little bar she knew not too far away from the restaurant.

They walked to it and got a small table. The place was bustling with Saturday evening customers. Conversation bubbled all around. Since they were sitting not too far from the bar, they had a good view of the area where bar loungers did the promenade for pickups.

But this was the sort of place where pickup lines usually included words like "my stockbroker" or "your 401K."

Ellis hated it immediately.

"I've never been here," he said.

"It's relatively new," Mallory said, looking around. "Like it?"

Carson didn't want to put a damper on the evening, so he decided against telling her he didn't like Yuppie/Buppie places. The whole outfit was filled with people who looked like they missed the '80s and were making up for it now. This was the L.L. Bean and Nordstrom crowd. But he could hang. He'd always been good at making the most of whatever situation he was in; even ones that left a bad taste in his mouth.

They put drink orders in, then settled back on a small loveseat to continue their conversation.

"So, tell me about your life," he said.

She smiled. "That's a question with a lot of scope. What do you want to know?"

With a glance around the lounge again, Ellis wondered how these rich people lived. Even though they'd had a nice dinner—well, nice as far as he was concerned—he was starting to resent Mallory her wealth and her privilege. A steakhouse probably wasn't her idea of a great place to go, not when a drink in this place probably cost as much as one of their dinners.

"Tell me about how you grew up," he said, as he focused his attention back on the woman and not the place.

Mallory smiled. "It wasn't perfect. I know that now, but I think I realized it even then."

"What was wrong?"

"I had the best of everything," she said. "You know, private schools, music, dance and language lessons, shopping trips to Paris. I got my first car, a Mercedes, when I was sixteen."

Carson rolled his eyes. "Oh, sure. That's every American kid's hard luck life. I'm supposed to feel sorry for you?"

Mallory scowled at him. "You don't get it," she said, trying to control both the exasperation and the frustration she felt. He was making light of something that was so serious, it had shaped her—and haunted her—all of her life.

"I didn't want *things,*" she said. "I wanted to be loved. The only reason my parents gave me stuff was to keep me out of their way, out of their lives." Mallory shrugged, the motion a sad sigh. "I suppose they thought if they kept me occupied with lessons and camp and shopping and vacations, I wouldn't recognize or realize how neglected I was. Mallory was a nuisance, a thing to be taken care of or gotten rid of when she was an inconvenience. The dogs got more attention than I ever did."

Carson felt sorry for her, even though he didn't want to. The more he got to know Mallory, the more he realized why she'd built such an impenetrable wall around herself. Like he'd been forced to do, for different reasons, of course, Mallory had learned to cope and survive in a hostile world.

She looked so pitiful sitting there that he found himself tempted to reach a comforting hand to her. Tempted, but not convinced.

He'd had lots of experience with actresses. They could turn on the tears and the sad stories better than anyone who'd ever won an Academy Award. But even as he thought the thought, something told him that Mallory wasn't acting—or at the least, she herself was convinced she'd had a rough time of it. She didn't know the meaning of hard times, though.

"I'd have given anything to have had a normal life," she said.

Carson smirked. "Including all the money?"

She lifted sad eyes to him. "Money isn't everything, Carson."

"Spoken exactly like someone who's always had plenty of it."

"You think I've never suffered?"

He sat back and crossed one leg over his knee.

"Oh, I'm sure you had to take ballet instead of tap lessons one year. Or maybe you broke a nail. Go on," he encouraged. "Tell me how it took you three months to find the perfect manicurist."

Mallory carefully placed her wine glass on the small table in front of them. "I guess it would have been too much to expect someone like you to understand."

She stood up, opened her small clutch handbag, and pulled out a crisp fifty-dollar bill. She dropped it on the table. "Good night, Carson."

His fists clenched in anger. He wanted to yell after her, call her a tease. He wanted to make her hurt as much as she'd hurt him. "Someone like you," she'd said. But that's what she would have expected. That's what she probably hoped—that he'd show his true color in her fancy little bar.

But Carson knew better. Not for a minute did he plan to fall for that poor little rich girl routine. Hell, she didn't know half the meaning of suffering! Women like her had never wanted for anything. Not one damn thing.

The waitress approached him. Carson saw her eye the fifty.

"What else can I get you, sir?"

"Just the check."

With another not quite subtle glance at the cash, the waitress nodded and slipped away.

Carson sat up and swore. Something about Mallory Heart brought out the worst in him. The fact that he wanted her like he'd never wanted a woman didn't help his disposition one bit. As a matter of fact, he regretted ever meeting her.

A couple of minutes later, the waitress returned. Carson handed her a twenty, more than enough for his beer and Mallory's glass of wine.

"Keep the change," he said, as he rose to leave.

The waitress's mouth dropped open. "This is seventy dollars," she said to his retreating back. "That's a lot of change."

Carson didn't even turn around as he stormed out the door.

Mallory refused to cry.

She refused to even acknowledge how much he'd hurt her. That Ellis Carson even had the power to hurt her infuriated Mallory. She'd never, ever, let anyone get under her skin. She'd survived emotional neglect and guilt trips from her parents. She'd survived a career setback that would have knocked other people down for the count. She'd done rounds with her cousin and emerged scratched but not defeated.

She'd even survived the trauma of knowing that the only reason guys ever, since high school, wanted to date her was because of her last name and the dollar signs that were attached to that name.

Through the years, Mallory's skin as well as her attitude had toughened. No one could hurt her if she didn't allow it. From inattention from her parents, inconsideration of her feelings from so-called friends, and the general thoughtlessness of men in general, she'd learned to cope with it all. She'd channeled and parlayed the anger into productive energy.

And then Ellis Carson came crashing into her world, making loud noises, rude comments, and attacking the very existence she'd painstakenly created. That assault angered Mallory. Instead of delving into the why of that, she dwelt on the anger. She let it feed and grow and fester.

Anger was a friend she knew and could handle.

The other confusing emotions were ones she didn't know and couldn't afford to investigate too thoroughly. They'd already managed to dull her senses to the point that she'd actually thought a connection had been made with that insufferable Carson.

Mallory had heard of people who let things like physical attraction, mutual interests, even love, distract them. She had no intention of falling for that sappy marketing stuff that greeting card companies thrived on. Mallory was about the real world.

"You should have known, Mallory," she told herself over and over again, as she practically stripped the gears on her Mercedes.

Driving fast always calmed her down. Her world in such turmoil, Mallory knew that a good drive would balance, and with luck, cancel out the bad stuff. She let the full power of the car unfurl as she drove faster, and faster still. The wind whipped her braids into a streaming trail behind her.

Mallory reveled in the speed, in the freedom, in the thought that the faster she drove, the faster she could escape the demon that chased her. The demon bore Ellis Carson's face.

She gritted her teeth and pushed the sports car to its limit, unaware of the tears that whipped from her eyes and disappeared in the breeze.

A blue and white flashing light in the rearview mirror caught her eye a few minutes later. Caught up in the drama of her heartache, the significance of those lights didn't dawn on Mallory until she saw a similar set coming across the interstate's grassy median headed toward her.

She cussed a blue streak as the state trooper behind her pulled in closer. Mallory didn't have to look at the speedometer to know she'd really done it this time.

Still cursing her stupidity, she flicked on her flashers to let the officers know she'd slow down as soon as she safely could.

Last time, the cop who'd pulled her over asked if her last name was Andretti or Gordon. This time they were going to lock her up and throw away the key. She already had so many points against her that she paid an arm and a leg for insurance. Not that the money mattered. But not having a license would.

As she brought the car and her emotions under

control, Mallory cursed the day she'd met Ellis Carson. This was all his fault. *All his fault.*

The state trooper in front of her cut her off as she finally slowed and stopped on the shoulder of the road. The other one pulled up behind her. Both troopers had weapons drawn as they carefully approached.

Mallory knew the routine—too well. She turned off the ignition and dropped the keys in the passenger seat next to her. With both hands on the steering wheel so they'd be in clear view of the officers, she waited for the inevitable.

Chapter 9

Ellis sat in his chair sulking. He'd been in a foul mood for the past week, ever since the argument with Mallory in her fancy little bar.

"Maybe you shouldn't have come over," Antwan said.

The boy sat on the floor across from Ellis. They were supposed to be playing Monopoly, but it hadn't been much of a game. Quandra returned from the kitchen with two bags of microwave popcorn.

With an uncertain glance at her brother, she handed Ellis a bag. "I put extra butter on yours, just like you like it," she told him.

When he didn't say anything, Quandra's lower lip trembled. She settled on the floor next to Antwan. Ray-Ray climbed down from his perch on the crate box sofa and joined his brother and sister.

Antwan decided to take some action. He stood and faced Ellis, his shoulders tight, his mouth a thin, angry line.

"Why are you taking it out on us? We didn't do anything to you."

"Huh?"

By now, quiet tears were falling from Quandra. She held the toddler Ray-Ray in her arms.

"What's wrong, Quan?" Ellis asked.

She looked at him, but didn't answer.

"Don't waste any tears on him," Antwan said.

As though a fog lifted in front of him, Ellis realized that the children were angry with him. He'd been unpleasant company at work all week; could he have been giving the kids the same treatment?

He sat up and forward on the chair and opened his arms to them. "I'm sorry, guys. It's been a hell of a week."

"Don't cuss in front of Ray-Ray," Quandra scolded, sounding a lot like a grownup.

"I'm sorry," he apologized.

Antwan wasn't so easily placated. "You promised you'd never be mean."

Ellis slid to the floor. Ray-Ray disengaged himself from his sister and settled himself in Ellis's lap. The three-year-old smiled up at him. Ellis hugged him close then kissed his forehead.

"You the man, Ray-Ray."

The toddler nodded then pointed to his chest. "I'm the man."

Hugging the child to him, Ellis grinned. But winning over the two older children would take more explanation. They were kids—Antwan, nine years old, and Quandra, seven. Unfortunately, they'd grown up much faster than children should. They'd seen their comfortable world turn upside down in the last few years. Antwan had a lot of lingering hostility—hostility that Ellis knew he had no business feeding.

He'd always been honest with them, though, particularly with Antwan. Now wasn't the time to change that policy.

"Remember when Michael from 3-B liked you, Quan?"

The girl nodded.

"But you didn't like him," he added.

"Yes, she did," Ray-Ray said. Then, making a kissing sound, the boy laughed.

Even Antwan smiled at that.

"I liked him, a little bit," Quandra admitted.

Ellis smiled. "Well, that's what's happened with me," he explained. "Remember how you were stomping around here, yelling at everybody?"

The girl nodded, then looked at her clasped hands.

"Well, you weren't mad at Twan or Ray-Ray or your

mom or me. You were frustrated about what was going on with Mikey, right?"

She nodded.

"So what you're saying is that you met a squeeze who got you tied up in knots?" Antwan asked.

Ellis scowled. Twan was sharper than a kid should be. "Yes," Ellis said. "But women are not squeezes. How many times do I have to tell you that?"

"Well, you roll up in here dissing us . . ."

Ellis cut him off with a hand in the air. "That's enough, Twan. I'm sorry I took my frustration out on you. That wasn't fair of me. It's never happened before, has it?"

"No," Antwan mumbled.

"Then why don't you cut me some slack?"

Quandra punched Antwan in the arm. "Yeah, cut the man some slack, Twan. Can't you see, he's in loooove." She fell over in a fit of giggles.

But Antwan saw a bigger issue on the horizon. "Are you gonna marry her and leave us?"

Ellis blinked, first trying to recover from Quandra's assessment and then reeling from Antwan's question.

Love? Marriage? With Mallory Heart?

Hah!

"That'll be the day," he muttered. The thought, however, was already worming its way through his system. He fought it, though, rebelling against it. All he wanted from Mallory was . . .

Well, . . .

He cleared his throat.

"Are you in love with her?" Antwan asked.

"In love with who?" a new voice asked.

Jeanette slowly made her way into the living room. She rubbed her extended belly as she walked. "Lord, this baby needs to hurry up and get here."

Ellis set Ray-Ray aside then hopped up to help Jeanette onto the sofa. He piled about three pillows on the sofa cushion then helped her ease onto them.

"Hand me those pillows," he said.

Quandra scrambled for two more pillows, which she then tucked behind her mother's back.

"Umm. Thanks, y'all," Jeanette said, as she rubbed her belly again. "Easy, child. Easy."

Ellis sat on the sofa next to her. He put a hand on her stomach. "Is he in there giving you fits again?"

Jeanette nodded. "None of you were like this," she told the three children.

"We were good babies, right?" Quandra asked.

"You sure were, precious. Who's winning the game?"

"Nobody," Antwan said. "We kind of stopped playing."

"You want your feet massaged?" Ellis asked Jeanette.

She smiled at him and patted his hand on top of her stomach. "I'm fine right now. Thanks, though."

Ellis pushed the game board aside then took the

throw pillow from the sofa and placed it on the crate coffee table. "Elevate."

Jeanette sighed. "Ellis, I swear. You're worse than the doctor."

He wiggled his hands in an up motion. She sighed, but complied. He eased first one leg up and then the other.

"Happy now?"

"Ecstatic," he said.

Ray-Ray climbed onto the sofa and settled in next to his mom.

"So," Jeanette said, "who is this who's in love?"

Antwan and Quandra glanced at each other.

"We were just talking," Antwan said.

His evasiveness wasn't lost on Jeanette. She looked at them, and then at Ellis. "Keeping secrets, huh?"

No one met her gaze. Jeanette chuckled. "That's all right, y'all. Be like that."

Ellis smiled. "Who wants pizza?"

A round of "I do" filled the small living room.

"Why don't you call it in, and I'll go pick it up? Who wants to go with me?"

Antwan and Quandra hopped up and headed for the door.

"You looked low on milk and bread. You need anything else?" Ellis asked Jeanette.

"You don't have to do all of this, Ellis."

He shook his head. "Yeah, I do." With that, he

leaned down, kissed her on the cheek, then headed outside to his truck.

Unable to sleep, Mallory slipped on a pair of purple bike shorts and a matching tank top. The deserted streets of Virginia Beach allowed her to drive fast and free. She'd tried to pay the most recent speeding ticket, but was ordered to show up in traffic court when she called to find out how much the fine would be. If the DMV wanted to haul her in to go to safe driving school or some such thing, they'd do it this time. In the meantime, Mallory decided she wasn't going to stress about it. She had more important things on her mind.

Things like Ellis Carson.

In the week since their disastrous dinner date, she'd made sure she was scarce when she thought he'd be working in the shop. She'd done a lot of work at home. Mallory had never avoided confrontation before, but this time prudence seemed the wisest course of action.

They'd seen each other twice. And both times, the politeness between them was so tight it was painful.

When she arrived at the shop, one car sat sentinel in the otherwise empty parking lot. Mallory pulled into a spot directly across from Mallory's Place, grabbed her briefcase and Evian, then headed into the only place where she knew she'd find solace.

The Quality Construction crew had made a lot of progress. Her vision was almost a reality. At the rate they were going, they'd be finished with everything in another week, almost two weeks ahead of schedule.

"He probably has them working double shifts to get done with me," she said.

While the fact remained that the only thing Ellis Carson wanted was to get her out of his business life, Mallory wondered if he'd spent sleepless nights wondering what their personal life together might have been.

She sighed. Her whole life had been nothing but a series of might-have-beens.

Building this store from the ground up gave Mallory an incredible sense of accomplishment—the significance of which she still couldn't make her mother understand. But that was one battle that she knew would continue to rage.

"It's my place," she said out loud in the empty space. "Mallory's Place. All mine."

A big grin spread across her face. A la a young Mary Tyler Moore, Mallory twirled in the middle of the floor, braids flying out all around her. She didn't have a cap to toss into the air, but her joy filled the place.

She laughed out loud at the thrill of it. Life was perfect. This moment was perfect. Her dream would soon be complete.

Wanting to remain surrounded by her dream, Mallory decided to work right there in the main room instead of sequestering herself in her office. She pulled a chair over and set up her laptop computer on one of the new countertops. Watching the construction crew during the day had given her an idea about the dressing rooms. Ned, the crew chief, had told her she'd have to get the changes cleared through his boss.

Mallory smiled. She liked Bailey. He'd proven easy to work with and accommodating of her suggestions. Unbidden, an image of that rude Ellis came to mind.

"He must be good at whatever it is he does," she muttered. If he weren't, he wouldn't have the unfailing devotion of his people.

Her experience in the Heart family stores and corporation had taught Mallory just how valuable unfailing devotion and loyalty could be. When it wasn't there, problems that were little could erupt into major disasters—like the one that had left her without a position in the deal she'd brokered for the family.

Thoughts of her cousin Cole and that entire fiasco gave her heartburn, so she banished that particular train of thought.

What's done is done, it's in the past. Next time do better. The words to the mantra she'd claimed as her own while in college ran through her mind. "That's just what I plan to do," she said out loud.

Despite her conflicted feelings toward Ellis Carson, which Mallory knew had more to do with her physical response to him than anything else, the businesswoman in her kicked in and could appreciate the way he ran his company. She didn't like to admit it, but she could learn some things from Ellis. She could use him as a case study.

All of her hand-picked employees would be chosen for their customer service savvy as well as their sense of style. The employee handbook she'd been writing would be an invaluable training tool, particularly when Mallory's Place grew into several shops and franchises.

Heart Department Stores stressed the importance of having a satisfied customer. It could take years to build a loyal customer and less than ten minutes to turn that same customer into a poster board of discontent that would then be spread far and wide.

"There'll be none of that at my place," she vowed.

Opening the word processing program, she started a file she labeled "Winning Difficult Customers." After thinking for a moment, she created a short outline that began, "Win the hardcase's confidence."

The following Monday, Mallory stood with Bailey in Mallory's Place. They were doing a walk-through. The majority of the work had, indeed, been completed. All that remained was laying tile and carpeting.

"It's beautiful," Mallory said. "Thank you."

"It's Carson you should be thanking," Bailey said.

Mallory frowned. "Yeah, well. Whatever."

Bailey considered her for a moment. "I heard about your date."

"I'll just bet you did. Did he tell you that he spent the entire evening goading me, making fun of me?"

"No. What he said was something like he really admired you."

That brought her up short. "I beg your pardon?"

Bailey smiled. He studied her for a moment.

Mallory watched indecisive expressions cross his face. He opened his mouth, then shut it, opened it again, and closed it. She sighed.

"Stop editing yourself and just say it," she said. "Whatever it is, I'm sure I've heard worse."

"You're too hard on yourself, Ms. Heart. Look at this place. It was all your vision."

Mallory eyed him. "That's not what you were about to say."

He shuffled his feet, then shyly glanced at her and shrugged. "You're right."

"Just tell me."

"It's not my place, Ms. Heart."

She opened her mouth to complain, but he held up a hand.

"It's not my place," he said. "But if I don't say something, it'll be on my head on Judgment Day."

"Judgment Day; isn't that a bit of an overstatement? We're talking about a retail boutique here."

"No," Bailey said. "I'm talking about two lives."

Mallory folded her arms. "Go on."

"I know you two didn't get off to a great start . . ."

"That's an understatement," she mumbled.

"But I don't think you should throw away what I see."

"Unless you're on a different channel, Bailey, the only thing you should be seeing is mutual animosity."

He shrugged. "I'll agree with the mutual part. But it's not animosity. The two of you have more in common than either of you realize."

"What could the poor little rich girl and the boy from the 'hood possibly have in common?"

"As I said, it's not really my place to say, but he's been . . ." Bailey paused for a moment searching for the right words. "The reason both of you are so hostile to each other," he began again, "is that you recognize that the opposite of all that hostility is intimacy. Both of you want it, but you're both afraid of it."

Mallory glared at him, the room temperature dropping a good thirty degrees. "And your degree in psychotherapy is from what school?"

Bailey picked up his clipboard from the counter where they stood. "The school of life, Ms. Heart. I graduated suma cum laude and majored in hard times. It might do you good to take a class or two."

"You can leave now," Mallory ordered, as she put both hands on her hips.

A sardonic smile tilted his mouth and Bailey shook his head. "I figured you'd say something like that. I'm leaving," he said. "But I'm going to leave you with this bit of advice. You're a very beautiful woman, Ms. Heart. I think you know that. I can see the beauty on the outside. But what's underneath? Whatever it is you're harboring inside your gut, it's eating you up. I saw what that same kind of emotional cancer did to Carson. I wouldn't want to see it happen to you."

With that, Bailey took his leave. Mallory stared after him, fuming. Stunned. Hurt. She nursed the hurt that had come with Bailey's simple truth.

Emotional cancer.

He'd hit it right on the head, although Mallory had never thought of her situation in quite that way. What did he see in her? Could other people see it or sense it? Did Ellis know her secret?

Slowly, as if in a daze, Mallory went to the large mirror overlooking the dressing area. She stared at her face, touched her skin, inspected her being. Could Bailey somehow see the emptiness she'd shielded all these years? The thought that she might be so easily read shook Mallory's foundation. She prided herself on keeping a distance, of not revealing too much of her true self or getting too close.

But if Bailey knew, did Ellis Carson know as well?

Chapter 10

Ellis crossed the street against the traffic. The check he'd been impatiently waiting for had finally arrived. Glad to have the money, he wanted the check deposited and growing interest as quickly as possible.

Everything was just fine in his world. It was a beautiful summer day. The bid for the fitness center project had been turned in on time. Mallory's store was all but finished, and Ned and Bailey could wrap up any loose ends there. He had another day's work to do before he completed the bid on the Knight & Kraus mall project, but that didn't include the time he needed to take to review what he'd done in the last week.

Carson Quality Contracting had a good shot of being the contractor on the company's new chain of stores. Ellis wanted to win the bid so badly he could taste the victory already. But first, he had to get the bid written. Being distracted by the thought of smoky eyes and long legs while working on that all-important bid didn't bode well. And now he needed extra time just to make sure he hadn't made any errors or miscalculations along the way.

Mallory Heart, in absentia, had managed to wreck his week as if she'd been right underfoot the entire time. He'd snapped at the office assistant, Sheila, been grumpy around the kids, and had been a general nuisance. All because of Mallory.

Bailey's taunt—"You got it bad, my brother"—didn't help Ellis's disposition.

"But this is a new day," he said. He held the bank door open for an elderly woman, then made his way to stand in the merchants' and business owners' line.

"Hi there, Mr. Carson. How's it going?" the teller greeted him, when it was finally his turn.

"Just fine. Super fine," he said, with a grin.

She smiled back as she processed his bank work. Within minutes he was back at his truck. The cell phone rang as he reached for his day planner.

"Carson Quality Contracting. How can I help you?"

"I was just calling to remind you about Pedro's court hearing," Sheila said.

"I've got it right here," Ellis said as he checked a notation in his planner. One of his men had gotten a traffic ticket and wanted a character witness when he went to court. Pedro was a good man, but Carson had his doubts about whether he'd get off on the charge.

"I'm on my way," he told Sheila. "Did Pedro wear a suit?"

"I think so," the office assistant told him. "Bailey was prepping him a little while ago. The poor guy is a nervous wreck."

"Well, he should be. Running three red lights in a row just to get home to watch 'E.R.' He's gonna get laughed out of the courtroom."

Sheila chuckled. "Maybe the judge is a fan, too. But you're going to be a terrific character witness for him. He'll get off with just a slap on the wrist."

"Let's hope so," Ellis said.

She gave him two messages that had come in since he'd left the office, then signed off. Ellis reached for the tie he kept in the truck and slipped it on. He quickly tied a Windsor knot then checked his handiwork in the rearview mirror. Satisfied, he headed to the courthouse.

Mallory prayed that no one she knew would be in the courtroom today. Her summons was to appear in Newport News, where, thankfully, she knew just a handful of people, mostly old-money friends of the Heart family. She'd decided to wear a softer-looking outfit than what she normally wore. The silk dress in a light peach color with pale green accents said, "I'm innocent." At least, that's what Mallory, bless her guilty soul, wanted to believe.

Opting against the family lawyer for this hearing, she slid alone into a seat near the front of the designated courtroom and watched humanity go by. The tales and the lies the judge heard made her want to laugh out loud: a nineteen-year-old tried to explain why he'd been driving with all of his lights off at three in the morning; a woman, about Mallory's age, cried when she admitted she'd been blow drying her hair with a cigarette lighter attachment when she'd rear-ended a minivan; and a man, who claimed he wasn't talking on his cell phone when he ran off the road and crashed his BMW into a tree, didn't have a prayer for leniency when his cell phone went off right in the middle of the judge's lecture.

Mallory mentally reviewed her own defense. She could say she'd had an argument with her boyfriend, but Ellis Carson could hardly be called her boyfriend. And this *was* a court of law where people were supposed to tell the truth, the whole truth, and nothing but the truth.

Your Honor, I was driving 105 mph in a 65 mph zone

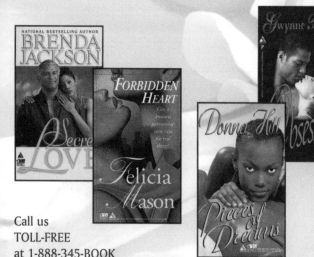

Accepting the four introductory books for $1.99 (+ $1.50 for shipping & handling, a total of $3.49) places you under no obligation to buy anything. You may keep the books and return the shipping statement marked "cancel". If you do not cancel, about a month later we will send 4 additional Arabesque novels, and bill you a preferred subscriber's price of just $4.00 per title (plus a small shipping and handling fee). That's $16.00 for all 4 books for a savings of 33% off the cover price. You may cancel at any time, but if you choose to continue, every month we'll send you 4 more books, which you may either purchase at the preferred discount price. . . or return to us and cancel your subscription.

THE ARABESQUE ROMANCE CLUB: HERE'S HOW IT WORKS

PLACE
STAMP
HERE

ARABESQUE ROMANCE BOOK CLUB
P.O. Box 5214
Clifton NJ 07015-5214

because I didn't want to admit to myself that I'd fallen for a man who in every way infuriates me—except, of course, Your Honor, when he's kissing the daylights out of me.

What was that? Oh, yes, Your Honor, I realize that speed limits are established to maintain safety on the roads. But you see, I drive fast to get rid of tension. Did you ever see the movie "Top Gun", Your Honor? Well, there's a lot of pent up sexual tension in there. And driving fast just lets it all out.

Six months in jail? Is that what you said, Your Honor? Hmmm . . .

The truth was the last thing Mallory had any intention of telling, at least not that version of the truth.

Wrapped up in her thoughts, she didn't hear her name called until someone tapped her on the shoulder.

"Hello, Mallory," Ellis said. "I think you're being summoned to the front."

He grinned down at her. Mallory wanted to slide right under the floor.

"What are you doing here?" she hissed.

"I could ask you the same question," he said. "Better get going. That bailiff doesn't look too friendly."

Mallory glanced at the bailiff, who was glaring in her direction. With a huff, she yanked her purse strap closer to her body and marched to the area in front of the judge.

Ellis watched her and grinned from his seat in the

gallery. She looked so angry, like a spitfire. Obviously, she'd never spent any time in a courtroom before. Humble was the way to approach these judges. Particularly if you were clearly in the wrong.

He waited to hear Mallory's charges and her self-defense. A few moments later, he realized she'd gotten the speeding ticket the night of their disastrous dinner.

"Serves you right," he mumbled.

Then a thought struck him. Mallory had been so upset about their conversation that she went speeding up the interstate. He'd played out that evening over and over in his head. Instead of baiting her, he should have been wooing her.

As he watched her and listened to the judge lecture her about excess speed and numerous tickets and unsafe driving, Ellis came to a realization. He'd dated his share of women through the years, but not one of them stimulated his intellect as well as the southern part of his body as much as this woman did.

When he sparred with her, he felt electrified. When he held her in his arms, he felt invincible. When he . . .

"Suspended for two months! You can't do that!"

The shriek echoed through the courtroom. People chuckled and pointed.

Ellis shook his head. "I thought rich people had lawyers who prepared them for this sort of thing," he mumbled to himself, embarrassed for Mallory.

"No, Miss Heart," the judge boomed back at her, "I can do that. And your outburst just earned you another month of a suspended license. At the end of your suspension, you will be required to attend the safe driving school. And if I see you in here again or see your name, you'll find out what it's like to sit in a jail. Understand?"

Mallory, her mouth a thin line, nodded. "May I ask a question?"

"What?"

"How am I supposed to get home and back and forth to work if I can't drive?"

The judge smiled a Grinchly grin. "That, Miss Heart," he began softly, "is something you should have thought about before you went tearing up Interstate 64 going 105 miles per hour." By the time he finished, he was practically yelling at her.

Whistles and "oooh's" went through the courtroom.

"Next!" the judge boomed.

Mallory's shoulders slumped. A deputy appeared beside her and led her to an area where she'd have to surrender her license.

Ellis sat back and folded his arms. "Damn, baby. You do believe in living on the edge with the volume all the way up, don't you?"

Pedro's case wasn't called next so Ellis slipped from his seat. He made his way to the area where people were to pay their fines and shoved his way through the crowd.

"Mallory," he called.

She turned around. Ellis froze.

The strong, invincible black woman he knew had been replaced by a vulnerable, tear-streaked stranger. Something in Ellis shifted, expanded. He wanted to protect her, to soothe her, to let her know everything was going to be all right.

He stepped forward, but paused, not sure how his presence and his empathy would be greeted.

Mallory's face crumbled. And in the next instant, she was in his arms, crying like a baby. He held her, rocked her, smoothed his hand down her back.

"It'll be okay. You'll see. Listen, we can work something out. Three months isn't so bad, Mal. Come on, baby, don't cry."

She kept right on crying, though.

So Ellis did what he was supposed to do. He continued to comfort her.

"Miss?"

She sniffed. "Yes?"

"Sign here, please."

Reluctantly, Ellis released her. She, too, seemed reluctant to leave the safety of his arms. She wiped her eyes, and Ellis found himself sorry he didn't carry handkerchiefs.

Mallory completed the paperwork, then handed

over her driver's license. New tears came at that. Ellis snaked an arm around her waist and held her close.

"It'll be all right," he said in her ear.

She sniffed and nodded. And then it was over.

He guided her back toward the courtroom.

"I can't go back in there," she said.

"Will you wait for me here, then? I can see you home. But one of my men is in there. I'm here to vouch for him. It shouldn't be too long."

Mallory nodded.

Ellis decided he liked the fiery Mallory much better than this defeated-looking waif. Maybe he could egg her on, get her blood and passion flowing again.

He opened his mouth to say something smart, then shut it. She'd been through a lot already. He didn't need to throw gasoline on the fire right this minute.

After seeing her to a seat, he dashed back to the courtroom to wait for his employee's case to be called. Within half an hour, Pedro's case was called and completed. He got off with a fine and a lecture from the judge. Seeing that it could have been worse, Ellis shook his employee's hand then quickly went to check on Mallory. She hadn't moved.

"Hey there."

She glanced up at him. "This is all your fault, you know."

Ellis grinned. The time alone had done its magic. The Mallory he loved was back. The grin fell off his face.

Loved? Mallory Heart? They hadn't known each other long enough for him to love her. Love her?

Ellis stared at Mallory for a long moment.

"What's wrong?" she asked, as she rose. "Is my mascara running down my face?"

"Huh? Uh, no. No. You look fine. Let's go," he said, taking her hand.

"I'm not going anywhere with you."

Ellis faced her. "Why does everything with you have to be an argument?"

"I'm not the one standing here making demands. I've just lost my license. I can't drive for three months. Do you know what an inconvenience that's going to be?"

But Ellis wasn't really listening to her. He was staring at her mouth.

"What?"

He snaked an arm around her waist and pulled her to him. When his lips covered hers, Mallory's argument and accusations died away. It was as though they were the only two people in the courthouse.

She pressed closer to him, her hand sliding across his crisp white dress shirt. His lips were warm and sweet on hers—delectable, like candy. It was a kiss her tired, abused soul needed for nourishment. She cherished the moment. Then she moaned when his growing erection pressed against her thigh. Her senses reeled as if short-circuited, and Mallory knew that this was meant to be. At this moment. With this man.

Forever.

"Let's go," he said.

This time, Mallory didn't object.

Chapter 11

Except for a call Mallory made to have one of the Heart family's aides pick up her car, the ride to her condo in Virginia Beach was quiet. They both realized that the rocky relationship they'd had up until this point was about to change.

At her place, Mallory turned on one light as she let him in.

"Make yourself comfortable," she said. "Would you like a drink?"

Ellis stopped her as she reached for another light switch. An arm curled about her waist and he pulled her to him. "No, Mallory. There's something I want far more urgently than a drink."

She licked dry lips and turned her head away from him a bit. "What is that?" she asked, her voice coming out shakier than she would have liked.

Lifting a finger, he stroked the braids closest to her face. "I think you know," he said. His head lowered.

Mallory twisted out of his embrace. "Let me get you a refreshment."

She dropped her bag on a small buffet table in the foyer and quickly disappeared. Ellis shook his head and walked deeper into the luxury apartment. His eyebrows rose at the dramatic art displayed around the main room. He wasn't a connoisseur, but he did recognize original oils and watercolors when he saw them.

"Definitely high maintenance," he assessed.

He ran a heel along the plush carpeting. Making love on the floor here definitely wouldn't qualify as a hardship. And make love to Mallory Heart was exactly what he wanted to do. He turned, looking for her.

She stood about ten feet away, quietly watching him.

"Nice," he said.

"Thank you."

When she didn't seem inclined to say anything else, Ellis took a step toward her. Mallory inhaled quickly. He paused.

"What's wrong?"

She fiddled with a braid, touched a chair, looked at everything except him. "I . . . This is . . ." She shrugged, unable to put into words the problem that plagued her.

Ellis erased the distance between them. He took her hands in his, surprised to find them cold.

"Having second thoughts?" he surmised, as he rubbed her hands between his.

"It's not you," she said.

He glanced to the left over his shoulder, and then to the right. "Hmm, seems like it's just us here. If it's not me, is it you?"

She bit her lip and nodded.

Ellis, tempted, leaned forward and kissed her. She warmed to the embrace, letting the moment ease her tension. His kiss, surprisingly gentle, helped her relax. He must have felt her tightly wound nerves relax because he softened the embrace even more. His lips continued to explore the velvety softness of hers then moved to the hollow of her neck.

Mallory moaned, and Ellis, in response, groaned.

"You make me impatient, woman."

"Is that good?"

Mallory felt his chuckle begin from deep within his chest. She felt his lips whisper across her ear. Mallory shuddered, the sensation one in which she found exquisite pleasure.

"Again," she murmured.

"Ummm, you like that, huh?"

Her braids, a cascade in his hands, became a weapon he used to tease her, to taunt her. With one thin braid in his hand, he traced the contours of her ear, the smooth lines of her neck, the hollow between her breasts. His hand followed suit, leaving a trail of heat and warmth and fire all along the way.

Tugging on his belt buckle, Mallory pulled him closer. "I feel so, so . . ."

At a lack for the right words, Mallory simply showed him how she felt by guiding his hand to her breasts and then lower. This time, it was Ellis who did the moaning.

"Bedroom," he murmured.

She took his hand and led him.

They eased out of the constriction of their clothes and Mallory opened her arms to him. They came together, tumbling onto the large canopy bed. Sheer panels draped overhead, framing them in a halo of sensuality.

Mallory explored the length and breadth of his body, traversing every inch of brown skin. She paused at numerous scars, kissing each one as though her touch could erase the old wounds.

"What happened here?" she asked, as she traced a thin line running along his ribs.

"Disagreement with a . . . Ahhh." His explanation cut off when her mouth followed the gentle journey of her finger.

When he could no longer stand her play, Ellis

slipped a condom on and turned the tables. He took his sweet time discovering all the hidden places that made Mallory moan. He licked the backs of her knees and ran a gentle hand up the insides of her thighs.

She writhed in sweet agony, even as a pressure mounted within.

"More," she moaned.

"Greedy little diva, aren't you?" he asked, with a chuckle. But the chuckle died away when her hand wrapped around his erection. She teased him, caressed him, fondled him until he parted her legs, ending the play.

She was taut and warm and . . . Ellis paused.

Mallory wrapped her legs around his waist. "Don't stop," she said, as her hands caressed his back. "Please."

He captured her gaze with his, his breathing ragged, forced, as he held out. For a long moment, they stared into each other's eyes.

"Please," she whispered, the entreaty a prayer, a wish, a promise.

And then he entered her.

"Why didn't you tell me?" he asked.

They lay together in the bed, Mallory's head on his chest, her hand tracing curlicues along his skin.

"You wouldn't have believed me," she said, simply.

Ellis sighed. "You're probably right."

"Was it really so bad?"

He sat up and pulled her alongside him. Taking her hands in his, Ellis kissed them. "Bad?" he repeated shaking his head. "Mallory, do you have any idea what just happened here?"

She looked down. "We had sex."

With one gentle finger he lifted her chin. He then traced the contours of her mouth with that finger. When he had her full attention, his mouth closed over hers. The kiss was renewal and life and thanks.

"No, Mallory Heart. We didn't merely have sex. You've granted me a gift that I didn't deserve. Why did you give it to me?"

Mallory shook her head. "You ask too many questions."

When she turned to scoot out of the bed, he stopped her. "Mallory, what we just shared here doesn't happen very often between two people. You made me realize that sex is sex. But lovemaking is something else completely. We made love here. And it was your very first time."

Mallory drew her legs up and clasped her arms around them. "So I was the oldest virgin in America. Is that a crime?"

Ellis watched her, wondering what was going on in her head. He was pleased—no, thrilled—that she'd waited. She had to have had other relationships. Why hadn't she slept with those men?

"No," he said, "being a virgin isn't a crime. But it's rare, particularly with someone your age."

"Now you make me sound ancient and foolish."

He wrapped an arm around her shoulders, easing her back against him. "You're not ancient or foolish," he said, as he planted tiny kisses on the bare skin of her shoulders. "You're beautiful and wise and . . ."

"Yes?"

He smiled at her impatience. "And a constant surprise to me."

Mallory tilted her head and they came together in a quiet kiss. His hands searched for pleasure points. When he cupped the fullness of her breast, Mallory sighed a whisper of satisfaction.

Before long they lay tumbled between her soft sheets, loving again. Mallory, a quick study, gave as good as she got and made Ellis cry out in ecstasy.

Much later, they sat together in the whirlpool in Mallory's very large bath, a bottle of champagne at the edge of the tub.

"Why me?" he asked.

"You keep asking me that," she said.

"That's because you haven't given me an answer yet."

Mallory closed her eyes for a moment, trying to collect her thoughts, which scattered with each touch from this man.

"Because," she finally said. "Because you make me feel alive and beautiful. And you didn't want me."

Ellis sat up. "What do you mean I didn't want you?" He reached for her hand and dragged it under the bubbling water to prove to her just how much he still wanted her.

"No," she said with a smile, as she caressed him. But before he sank into sweet oblivion, she pulled away. "Not that kind of want."

He shifted and reached for the glass they shared. "Explain then."

Mallory stretched her legs out, tangling them with his. "All my life, I've been the rich girl. The one who had everything. I had everything I could possibly want except for the one thing I wanted most of all."

"What was that?"

She glanced away. "Someone to love me for me—not for what I would bring to a partnership or marriage. Not what my trust fund or bank balance or portfolio showed. I wanted someone, anyone, to just love me for who I was."

"That's what you were trying to tell me that night," he said.

Mallory nodded. "It seemed so easy for other people, other girls, to fall in love, marry the man they loved, and settle down with families and even careers. But not for a Heart. All of us are like this. Messed up on the inside. We keep therapists on retainer, you know."

He smiled at her humor, then reached to refill

their champagne flute. He handed it to Mallory, who sipped before giving it back to him.

"My parents thought I was sleeping with every guy in school just to spite them. I think they waited for me to come home pregnant and say that the father was the chauffeur or something."

"But you didn't sleep around," Ellis said. "Most girls would have."

She smiled. "You forget. I'm not most girls. I've always been my own person. I've always gone against the grain, set my own trends, and followed my own path. I figured that the only thing I truly had of value to give someone was myself. And I decided to be greedy and keep all the goodies for me."

Ellis laughed out loud at that. "Well, I, for one, Mallory Heart, am glad you finally decided to share."

"You never asked anything of me," she said. "And you fought me at every turn."

"And this is what turns you on? Okay, let's see. What can I say to make you angry?"

She splashed water on him, then rose from the whirlpool and reached for a towel.

"Mercy," he whispered, as he watched her. The memory of those long legs wrapped around him was all the catalyst his body needed to again harden and ready itself for her.

"I beg your pardon?" she said.

"If you don't put some clothes on we might just see what this marble feels like."

Mallory's smile, like Eve's, held temptation and promise. Slowly, she dropped the fluffy white towel until it draped at her feet. Ellis rose from the tub and came to her.

Chapter 12

"What happens now?" Mallory asked.

"You tell me," he said. "What do you want to happen now?"

Mallory studied him. They sat at the table in her eating room, dining on omelettes with strawberries and champagne. She'd let him into her life, into her sanctuary, into her body. And now she didn't know what to do with him.

"I don't know," she answered.

He looked up from his plate, then put his fork down. "There are a couple of ways this can go," he said. "We can pretend it never happened, that this was just one of those spontaneous moments, you know, the kind where you're so curious you just have to find out what the candy tastes like."

She raised an arched eyebrow at him and frowned.

"Or," he quickly added, "we can just kind of go with the flow."

"What is this go-with-the-flow like?"

He looked at her, his expression quizzical. "Have you never been in a dating relationship, either?"

"I've dated," she snapped.

"But nothing long-term," he surmised.

"I haven't had time for long-term," she said. "I've been busy working, first in the family business and now for myself."

"I see," he said, rubbing his chin.

"What does that enigmatic 'I see' mean?"

"First, you tell me what enigmatic means."

Mallory flushed. Standing quickly, she changed the subject. "Would you like coffee?" she asked, as she headed to the kitchen. "I can grind some beans for espresso if you'd like."

Ellis wiped his mouth with his napkin and stood up. "I think it's time for me to go."

She looked up. "Enigmatic means mysterious or puzzling."

He shook his head. "It's not about fancy words, Mallory."

She folded her arms. "Then tell me what it is about."

He waved a finger between the two of them. "Us. You and me. We're from two different worlds."

"And?"

"And this will never work."

Her hands made their way to her hips. "And just what is this 'this' you refer to?"

"Mallory, the sex between us is fabulous . . ."

"You said it wasn't sex, that it was something more," she said, quietly.

He sighed. "It is. But we just don't communicate the same way."

"What do you want, Ellis? Do you want me to wave a hand and—Pouf!—have all my money disappear? It doesn't work like that. Money is just another burden to bear."

He shook his head. "That's exactly what I mean. To you, money is a burden. To the people in my world, money is a savior."

Her shoulders slumped. "So, it's over. Is that what you're saying?"

Ellis ran a hand over his moustache then rubbed his eyes. "No."

"Then what? Talk to me." Mallory didn't particularly care for the desperation she heard in her voice. But her gut was telling her that if he walked out of her house tonight, he'd walk out of her life forever. She hadn't waited this long to give herself to someone only to discover after it was too late that she'd made a horrible mistake.

Mallory allowed no margin for error or mistakes in her life. She'd made one and had no intention of ever facing failure again. Not if she had any say in the matter.

Ellis faced her, palms flat on the kitchen counter. "You want to know the truth?" he asked.

She nodded.

"Well, the truth," he said, with a wave of a hand around her condo, "the truth is I could never give this to you. I make a decent living because I work hard. I have people to take care of, people who depend on me. I don't waste resources on fancy coffee beans or," he added with a nod toward the breakfast table, "drink Dom Perignon for breakfast."

"I thought it was a nice touch."

He sighed. "It is, Mallory. But it's the sort of thing I could never provide for you. What kind of life would someone like you have with someone like me?"

"Is that a proposal?"

His eyes widened. "What?"

"Is that your way of making a backdoor proposal?"

"I'm not proposing anything," he declared. But Mallory saw the lie in his eyes.

She realized with sudden clarity that it was fear that had him in the corner he now saw himself in. His thoughts *had* been on the what-next of the what-if.

Mallory came from around the island and took both of his hands in hers. "The only thing we have to fear is not stepping out on what we believe," she said.

"What's that, some New Age mumbo jumbo?"

She smiled as she lifted his hand to the area near her heart.

"No, Ellis Carson. It's a woman talking to a man. Today, I stepped out into a territory that was uncharted for me. Was I afraid? You betcha. But I believed in what was at stake. I wanted to share with you, to be with you, to make love to you and with you. And now, all I'm asking—no," she paused. "All I'm saying is that there seems to be something here. I don't know what happens next, but I'm willing to take the step out on faith to find out what it might be. Are you?"

He paused then nodded, pressing a kiss onto her hands.

At dinner the following night, this time in a restaurant of Mallory's choosing, they established the rules of engagement for their courtship: no one-upmanship, mutual agreement on where they'd dine or go out, and open lines of communication as the biggie.

The next few weeks passed in a blur. Mallory and Ellis dated the way normal people dated. And they argued about everything from local politics and whether men should still hold doors open for women to whether it was proper to tip flight attendants for excellent service and which one of them should pay for their dates.

The day Mallory met Big Mama remained emblazoned in her mind. The older woman, who was about four foot eleven and just barely one hundred pounds, sized Mallory up in an instant.

"She's the one, Ellis. Hurry up and marry her before you do something that ticks her off."

Mallory blushed from the top of her head to the soles of her feet. Ellis shuffled his feet and cleared his throat.

"Why y'all acting all shy now? I know you done done the dance between the sheets. You can tell it just looking at ya'."

"Big Mama," Ellis whined.

"What? You knows I speak the truth. The Good Lord don't like that pressing the flesh before the vows, so y'all just need to hurry up with it. Bring me some great-grands."

Mallory choked on her sweet roll.

Great-grands! Good grief! Mallory had no intention of bringing any illegitimate children in the world. Mallory's father and uncles had seen to enough of that. The Heart family was crawling with half-cousins and whatnot. While the Hearts eventually took care of those they accepted into the family, it was an eye-opener to view the notion of family and children from Big Mama's perspective.

"Babies are to be loved and cherished," she told them.

With the exception of her cousin Cole, who'd been

adored by their grandmother all his life, Mallory had no experience with the notion of people being cherished. People, in her family's eyes, were commodities, even pawns.

"So y'all go on and hurry it up with the vows," Big Mama said. "I plans to be sittin' in the front row, you know. I gets a little tear in my eye at weddings. Now if ya'll was doing right, like the Good Book says, the kissing and the pressing of the flesh don't come 'til after the preacher man says 'you may now kiss the bride.' "

Ellis managed to hustle Mallory out of Big Mama's house before she launched into a full sermon about fornicating. That had been two nights ago. And Mallory still blushed when she thought about the meeting with the woman who'd raised Ellis. They'd been very careful about contraception, so no great-grands were likely to be on the way. But Mallory had at odd times found herself thinking about what it might be like to give birth, to be a mother—to bear Ellis Carson's children.

She smiled at the thought.

"I'd be a better mom than my mother ever was," she said.

"Beg pardon, Ms. Heart?"

She glanced up at Bailey, who'd just walked into the outer office of Carson Quality Contracting. Mallory and Ellis had a lunch date and Mallory had arrived early.

"Nothing. I was just talking to myself," she said.

"So, how are things going?" Bailey asked.

"You mean you don't already know?"

He chuckled. "Carson's a private man, ma'am. If you're worried about your secrets being broadcast, you can rest easy. All he'd tell me was to mind my own business."

Mallory's smile widened in approval. "Good. And in answer to your question, everything is just fine, thank you very much."

"Well, not everything," Bailey said. "He sent me to pass along some bad news."

Anxious, she gripped Bailey's arm. "What's happened?"

"He's fine. We just have a problem at a job site. He's going to have to work through lunch. I just came back to pick up some paperwork that we need out there."

"Oh," Mallory said, disappointment clouding her voice.

"There's a but, Ms. Heart."

"I beg your pardon?"

He grinned. "Just a saying, there's a but, you know."

She looked at him blankly.

He cleared his throat. "Carson wanted to know if you'd meet him for dinner. He said you'd know the place."

Mallory smiled. One of their agreements was that

if either had to break a date because of work, the one who broke the date would treat the other to his or her favorite restaurant. Mallory's mouth already watered at the thought of going to her favorite Continental restaurant. Ellis hated it, which made her all the more gleeful.

"Tell him I'll meet him there at eight."

Bailey dropped some envelopes on the desk for Sheila. "Will do. Have a good time."

Mallory reached for her handbag and went to the open office door to say farewell to Sheila. On her way out, she glanced at the envelopes Bailey'd left on the desk. The Knight & Kraus logo leaped out at her.

She frowned and glanced back at the office where Sheila was filing paperwork. Mallory edged a manila envelope out of the way to get a better look at the Knight & Kraus envelope in their trademark blue on brown vellum. The letter was addressed to the construction company, with attention to Ellis.

It was probably a credit application, she decided. While she had lots of issues with the low-life scum that ran the Knight & Kraus stores, she couldn't fault someone for wanting to establish a line of credit with them. They did, after all, have a division that specialized in work clothes.

Letting the matter go, Mallory left the construction company office and went to the car, where Consuela, pressed into chauffeur duty, was waiting to take her back to Mallory's Place for the afternoon interviews with prospective employees.

"Why'd you decide to have dinner with me?" Ellis asked her.

"What? And miss out on the opportunity to see you scowl and frown and complain about this place?"

He smiled. "It's not *that* bad," he admitted. Then, after a moment, "You're my kind of woman, Mallory."

The corners of her mouth tilted up as she cocked her head regarding him. "Okay, I'll bite. What kind of woman is that?"

Leaning forward, Ellis took one of her hands. With his thumb, he softly caressed her palm. "The kind whose hands are soft, but whose mind is quick. The kind of woman who appreciates the finer things in life . . ." He paused.

"Yes?"

"Yet who values life."

Mallory smiled, but the gesture seemed sad. "You had to edit your comment. When are you going to trust me enough to just say what's on your mind?"

Honest, Ellis dipped his head to her. "Yes, I did edit. And I do trust you, Mal. But I also know how fragile you are."

She frowned. "I've been called many things in my time, but fragile is not one of them."

"That's because they don't see you like I do."

That compliment humbled her. She still, however, wanted to know what he'd been about to say before he changed his mind and said the nice thing. Gazing at him, she raised an eyebrow.

Ellis chuckled. "You just like to fight, right?"

She nodded. "It's exhilarating."

"So are some other things," he said, as his gaze took a dip to her breasts.

"Stop changing the subject."

He sighed. "Mallory, you've never known what it's like to need. So it's difficult to explain some things to you. There is, you know, a difference between need and want."

"I know that."

"I know you do," he said. "But . . ."

She cut him off. "There is no but, this time, Ellis. No, I've never needed shoes on my feet or food on my table. I've never wondered what it might be like to rob Peter to pay Paul. But I do know need. There are some basic human needs that I've done without for so long that it wasn't until . . ." she shrugged, as her words trailed off. "Well, it wasn't until lately that I realized just how much was missing from my life—just how hollow my existence has been.

"Deep down, of course, I've always known. But it's easy to mask the pain of need when you have the resources to numb that pain with material possessions."

"You keep talking about this, so why don't you explain things to me. Tell me about it," he invited.

Mallory shook her head as she pulled a bit of bread from a dinner roll and nibbled on it. "We tried that already," she said. "If you'll remember, the conversation ended in an argument that eventually led me to losing my drivers' license."

Nodding, Ellis conceded the point. "That was because I was letting my own stuff get in the way of hearing you."

Mallory ate the other piece of bread. After chasing it down with a sip of wine, she decided to turn the tables on him. "What are your issues?"

He grinned. "You just want to know my stuff so you can use it against me."

She reached for his hand. "No, Ellis Carson. I want to know your 'stuff,' as you call it, so I can know you."

For a long time, the space between them remained quiet, contemplative, as they assessed each other. This moment had the power to determine all their future moments. They each recognized that. Careful to make the right decision, the time and the silence grew—not in an uncomfortable way, but one that deepened the bond between the unlikely pair.

Ellis took her other hand in his so that they were joined across the table. "What forbidden spell are you casting over me, Mallory Heart?"

She didn't smile as she gazed into his eyes. "The same one you've put on me."

At that, Ellis did smile. He lifted her right hand and kissed the back of it. A moment later, he released both of her hands and sat back in his chair. A waiter appeared and removed their dinner plates then promised to return with the dessert cart.

"I was sent down here to live with my grandmother when I was twelve," Ellis began. "Big Mama ran a tight ship. She didn't have a lot of money, but she had a lot of love and a direct line to Jesus."

Mallory smiled.

"That woman had me in church for Wednesday night prayer meetings, Friday night praise, and all day Sunday service."

"You had more church in a week than I had my whole life. My family is officially Catholic, but no one practices or goes to Mass."

"Well, in Big Mama's house, it was her way and God's way or the highway."

"And you needed that?" Mallory asked.

"Big time. In New York, where I'm from, I was on my way to becoming an original gangster. I'd been in juvie hall twice when my mom said 'that's enough.' Before I knew what had happened, I was shipped south for some home training Big-Mama-style."

"Did she succeed?"

Ellis stared at her for a moment. "You tell me. I own my own business, one I came to as a carpenter's assistant. I saved my money and eventually bought out the owner. I do close to two million in work every year." He shrugged. "I didn't finish college, but I know the value of education. I take care of my own, and that includes Big Mama."

"I've never had a sense of community," Mallory said.

"It's not something you can buy."

Pain flashed across her face.

"I didn't mean it like that," he quickly assuaged. "Community isn't a place, Mallory. It's a state of mind. There were many nights when we had rice and beans for dinner and rice for breakfast. But our clothes were always clean and pressed. There were hugs and lessons about people who didn't have it as good as we did.

"Big Mama made it her business to take care of people in need," he said. "It never crossed her mind or even dawned on her that she was one of them. When the church gave away government cheese and bread, Big Mama always took half of what we got and gave it to somebody else."

"Didn't you feel cheated?"

Ellis shook his head. "You're not getting it. We didn't have fancy cars. We didn't live in a grand house. And we didn't have all the stuff that Americans use to define success and wealth. But we were successful and wealthy in the ways that mattered. Of course, it took me these thirtysome years to appreciate it all. Don't think that I was always as wise as I am now."

She smiled. "I wouldn't presume to think such a thing."

"Watch it now."

They grinned at each other.

"So where is Big Mama now?"

Ellis glanced at his watch. "Probably at church praying for her backsliding grandson."

"So you need prayer, huh?"

"Reverend Gordon, the preacher, used to say 'we've all sinned and come short.' "

The waiter appeared before Mallory could answer. The dessert tray, filled with a delectable assortment of sweet temptations, had Mallory's full attention. She selected a chocolate mousse. Ellis's pager went off as he pointed to a deep dish apple pie.

"With ice cream," he told the waiter, as he glanced at the small black box at his side. Frowning, he pulled the pager up, read the alpha numeric message, and then swore.

"What is it?" Mallory asked.

"Something important. We need to go. Do you mind?"

She glanced in the direction the waiter had disappeared, then turned back to him. "No. It's all right. I can call a cab."

"I picked you up," Ellis snapped. "I'll take you home." His tone told Mallory this wasn't a good time to argue.

"Okay," she said, hoping to avoid a scene.

He motioned for the waiter, canceled their dessert order, and asked that he hurry up with the check. Mallory winced at his tone. Their service had been excellent thus far. Ellis didn't have to go ghetto on her now.

Ellis was standing and waiting when the waiter returned with their bill. Without a word, Ellis whipped out enough cash to cover the amount with a tip. His pager went off again. He grabbed it in one hand and Mallory's in the other.

"Come on," he said, half dragging her out of the upscale restaurant.

"Ellis, my goodness. You're acting like the place is on fire."

He didn't pause in his stride to his truck. When he made no effort to help Mallory into the cab, she frowned at him, then tried to hoist herself up. She lost a high-heeled mule the first time.

Ellis started the engine and reached for the cell phone. "Come on, Mallory. We gotta get going."

"If you'd just give me a moment," she called up to him. Tossing her shoe into the cab first, she managed to scramble up. She'd barely pulled the seat belt over when he tore out of the parking lot, steering with one hand and punching numbers on the cell phone keypad with the other.

After a moment, he barked his name, cell number, and location to the person on the other line. "Send an ambulance to the thirteen hundred block of 16th Street in Newport News," he said.

"What's wrong? What happened?"

He ignored her as he gave the person a woman's name, Jeanette, and other vital information. The grim expression on his face told Mallory two things: the situation was serious, and he cared about the woman very much. While she couldn't claim even a bit of knowledge about religion and had no religious upbringing on which to draw, Mallory prayed that the grandmother he obviously loved so much would be all right.

Ellis sped through the Hampton Roads Bridge-Tunnel then took the exit off the interstate that led to downtown Newport News. Mallory glanced at the speedometer. Had *she* been behind the wheel, every state trooper in the region would have been out on patrol. But without a single one of the State Police cars in sight, Ellis zipped along at a serious clip.

"Is there anything I can do?" Mallory asked.

He glanced at her then took her hand in his and squeezed it.

"Pray," he said. "Pray that they're gonna be okay. That's what I'm doing."

They? Mallory wondered. But she didn't question him, his mind and attention obviously elsewhere.

Within minutes they pulled into a dilapidated-looking apartment complex. The sign said Banneker Court.

Mallory had heard about poor neighborhoods and had seen glimpses of them on the television news. But she'd never actually been in one. She glanced at the expensive watch and bracelets on her wrist and wondered about the H.Stern emeralds on her ears and at her throat. The deep green of the earrings and pendant matched the tunic blouse she wore over a pair of stretch pants. Every fiber in her being itched to remove her conspicuous evidence of wealth. But she waited, wanting to take his cue without giving offense.

A crowd gathered in front of one of the buildings watching an ambulance with flashing lights back closer to the door of one of the apartments.

"Stay here," he ordered. Without waiting for a response from her, Ellis was out of the truck and running to the apartment.

Mallory quickly locked both doors, then looked around. The people, all curious, talked among themselves, some smoking, others wearing anxious expressions as they watched the apartment. A pregnant woman wearing a skin-tight orange bodysuit held a toddler in her arms. Another woman with a head full of pink and green rollers gestured with a cigarette as she talked to a couple of men. A group of children, oblivious to the commotion, played in a dirt-packed area that was obviously supposed to be a playground.

Mallory shuddered. *Is this how other people really lived?*

She had a hard time coming to grips with the sight

of the humanity just beyond the relative safety of Ellis's truck. She'd never given poor people one thought. Any philanthropic efforts she participated in were made through the family's charitable trust that was run by one of her bleeding-heart cousins. Mallory wasn't even sure which one.

As she wondered what it might cost to supply the children with some decent playground equipment, a second ambulance screeched to a halt near the first one. Paramedics lifted a gurney into the first one, shut the door, and sped off.

Ellis appeared at the apartment door, yelling something to the driver of the second ambulance. With the windows up, Mallory couldn't hear him, but she did recognize the way people deferred to him. As the emergency medical technicians dashed into the apartment, a little girl appeared at Ellis's side. Mallory leaned forward, trying to get a better view.

His daughter? She wondered. *No, maybe a niece.*

He'd said he took care of his own, but he hadn't exactly specified or enumerated just how many "his own" meant or who they might be beyond his grandmother, Big Mama.

Suddenly, Mallory realized she knew very little about Ellis Carson; or at least very little that mattered in her world. She was about to pull out her StarTac to call for a driver when Ellis appeared at her door. He yanked on the handle, but nothing happened.

He banged on the window. "Open the door, Mallory."

She quickly complied, but hesitated about moving.

"Let them in," he said. "They'll sit in the middle."

They who?

But before she could put voice to the question, he stepped aside. Two children, a boy and the girl she'd seen, stood close by. The boy looked to be about nine or ten, and even Mallory could tell he desperately tried to keep a brave front. The girl, however, had tears running from her eyes as she clung to Ellis.

"Come on, Mallory. Let them up," he prompted.

She slid from the cab, careful about her shoes. The kids hopped up as if they did it everyday. Mallory stared after them. When they were settled, Ellis helped her back into the cab, then dashed to the apartment again, leaving Mallory alone with the two children.

Glancing at them, the boy stony-faced, the girl softly crying, Mallory seemed at a loss. She looked through the windshield to see what Ellis was doing. The EMTs had wheeled a second gurney from the apartment. Ellis bent over the person on the stretcher and said something, a moment before the paramedics hoisted it up into the back of the ambulance.

A moment later, Ellis hit the door and the emergency rescue vehicle sped away. Beside Mallory, the girl, watching the scene, whimpered. Mallory had never been around children. She didn't know what to do. Her own mother had been no model parent. All of Mallory's tears had been wiped away by Consuela. It had been Consuela who comforted her when she was sick or when her distracted parents did something they didn't realize hurt their daughter. It was from Consuela's love and attention that Mallory drew.

Maneuvering so she could put her arm around the girl, Mallory twisted to the left, leaving a small pocket between them that would nestle the child's head.

"It's going to be okay," she assured the girl, even though she had no idea if that were really the case. "Shh, it'll be all right, you'll see."

As the girl settled into her embrace, Mallory could feel the youngster's hot tears soaking into her tunic blouse. In the midst of the girl's despair though, the value of the tunic diminished and something in Mallory expanded. What was most important was enveloped in her arms.

Chapter 13

"What happened, Twan?" Ellis asked.

Following the ambulance, Ellis was making his way through the city streets, headed to the hospital. Mallory still held the girl nestled in her arms.

"Ray-Ray was running around in the playground when he got sick. He was hurtin' real bad," Antwan said. "TiNisha carried him back to the 'partment. Mama gave him some medicine and made him lie down. But he didn't seem to get any better. That was yesterday," the boy added.

"What happened today?"

"This morning, Mama took him to the clinic and we stayed with Miss Juanita."

"I shoulda checked on him sooner," the girl whimpered.

"It's not your fault, Quandra."

"Yes, it is," she wailed. "It was my turn to be responsible."

Above the children's heads, Mallory and Ellis glanced at each other.

Antwan patted his sister's knee, a comforting gesture not lost on Mallory. "It's all right, Quan," he said. "It's all right. Ray-Ray's gonna be okay."

Ellis had to stop for a light. His impatience manifested itself in thumping on the steering wheel. He glanced at Antwan. "What happened after the clinic?"

"Mama said she wasn't feeling well, that she was kinda tired. Her back hurts all the time. So she went to lay down after she put Ray-Ray to sleep."

"She told me to check on him every thirty minutes, but I forgot," the girl burst in.

"It's okay, Quandra. You did everything you were supposed to do."

Mallory's gaze met Ellis's, her question evident in her eyes.

"Ray-Ray has sickle cell," Ellis explained. "He's having a really bad pain episode right now."

Mallory had a thousand questions, chief among them being Ellis's relationship to the children. They obviously knew, trusted, and loved him. But now wasn't the time. She could, however, find out their names. The boy had been called Antwan and the girl, something that sounded like Kwan. Since Ellis didn't seem inclined to make any introductions, she took the initiative.

"My name is Mallory," she told the girl.

"Oh, yeah," Ellis said. "Mallory, this is Antwan, my main man. And the beauty in your arms is Miss Quandra."

Mallory smiled at the compliment he gave the girl, noticing how Ellis boosted Quandra's self-esteem by affirming her in the presence of others. There was definitely more to Ellis Carson than met the eye. Mallory snuggled the girl closer to her.

The four rode the rest of the way in silence. Ellis had them get out at the emergency room entrance while he parked the truck. Minutes later, he took charge. Impressed despite herself, Mallory watched him command and receive the same type of respect her wealthy uncles and relatives assumed as their birthright.

She'd learned a lot about Ellis tonight; and every bit of it just increased her opinion of him. As she watched him answer questions and fill out paperwork, Mallory realized just how easy it would be to fall in love with this man. For so long, she'd held her heart in check, and the loosening of her heartstrings came as something of an emotional surprise.

Thinking back to what Bailey accused her of falling

victim to—emotional cancer—Mallory realized she liked this new feeling much better than the hollow emptiness she'd carried around like luggage all these years.

"Why don't you all wait over there," Ellis said. "I'll just be a few more minutes."

"I want to see Mom," Antwan said.

"What about Ray-Ray?" Quandra asked.

"I'm sure the doctors will let us know," Mallory gently said. "Come over here with me. We'll wait together. And see, we'll be able to see the emergency room from there," she said, pointing out the proximity of the waiting room to the ER.

Ellis gave a grateful smile to Mallory and nodded to Quandra. When the girl took her hand, Mallory let out a breath she hadn't realized she'd been holding. Never in her life had Mallory been a caregiver or a comforter, so the latent skills seemed all the more remarkable. And, she'd been accepted by someone who knew nothing about her background, even though that someone was a child. That, alone, made Mallory feel good about herself.

With Antwan leading the way for the women, the three made their way to the family waiting area.

Antwan and Quandra sat huddled together, anxiously awaiting word about their mother and brother. Mallory sat quietly, contemplating things Ellis could only wonder about. The doctors had been working on Ray-Ray for about an hour and they still hadn't had word about his condition. A while ago, a nurse had come to tell him Jeanette was doing okay. They had her hooked up to a fetal monitor though, and it would be a little while. Her pressure was way up and that wasn't good.

Ellis looked at Mallory. She'd been a trooper all night long.

"Not exactly the most romantic date, is it?"

She smiled and reached for his hand. "Actually, it has been," she said. "You've made me realize some of the things that are missing in my life."

"Like what?"

"Well, for starters," she said, "a life."

He squeezed her hand. "You have a life, Mallory. It's just different from mine."

In a reflective mood, she raised his hand to her mouth and kissed the back of his palm. "Yours has people and lives and passion in it. Mine has, well . . ." She shrugged. "Are Antwan and Quandra your children?"

Before he could answer, though, a nurse in scrubs appeared and announced that they could see Jeanette. The children hopped up and raced ahead, even though they didn't know where they were going. Hand-in-hand, Ellis and Mallory followed the nurse.

The reunion was a mix of tears and laughter. Quandra, assured yet again that she'd done nothing wrong, refused to leave her mother's side. Mallory hung back a bit, not wanting to intrude, but curious nonetheless.

"You must be the secret lady," the woman said from her hospital bed.

Mallory stepped closer. Then her mouth dropped open. This wasn't Big Mama. The woman in the bed was just a few years younger than she was and was pregnant. Very pregnant.

Bile rose in Mallory's throat. She'd been played! She turned to glare at Ellis, but his back was to her as he quietly talked with a nurse. All this time she'd been worried about a grandmother, someone old and cherished and wise.

This woman was none of those things. Not a single one of them.

The woman placed a protective hand over her stomach then pushed herself up with the other. "I'm Jeanette," she said, after she got settled.

"Mallory," she said. "Mallory Heart."

Jeanette's eyebrows rose as she took in the fancy clothes and jewelry on Mallory. "Heart, like the stores?"

Mallory nodded.

"Wow." She shook her head. "Wow. And you were watching my kids. Thank you."

Part of Mallory wanted to respond kindly; the other, insecure part of her needed some answers.

"Oooh," Jeanette said, and she paused, her face scrunched in pain. "That one hurt."

Mallory cast an anxious gaze toward Ellis and the nurse, but both had slipped from the area. "Do you need a doctor?"

Jeanette chuckled as she shook her head. "I just need this linebacker in here to settle down. This boy is something else," she said, rubbing her stomach. "Want to feel?"

Mallory recoiled. A shadow crossed Jeanette's face.

"Sorry," the younger woman mumbled.

Feeling chagrined, Mallory stepped forward again. "It's not . . . I'm not good in hospitals and around sick people."

That brought an outright laugh from Jeanette. "Sister-friend, I'm not sick. Just pregnant. And if Ellis here will cooperate, it'll be another few weeks before he makes his appearance."

Mallory blanched. "Ellis?"

Jeanette nodded and smiled. "That's the name we decided on. If the baby grows up like Carson, he'll be a good man. Ellis is real good with kids. Loves 'em to death. He's a good man, that he is."

Something in Mallory shriveled and died in that instant. He'd slept with her, made love to her . . . and then went home to his family. Realizing just what "his own" really meant, Mallory felt like a fool. He'd willingly taken what she'd offered, all the while knowing that . . .

She cut her thoughts off, suddenly blinking back

tears. But Mallory was strong. She refused to cry, and definitely not in front of Ellis's pregnant girlfriend.

"Excuse me." With all the dignity she could muster, especially seeing how she felt like a used dishrag, Mallory walked from the hospital emergency room area. She walked down the corridor and straight out the door.

Not until she was outside in the still, summer night did she let the tears start to fall. A cab unloading two elderly women was at the curb. Mallory dashed for it before the driver could get away. She motioned to the driver, who nodded as he helped the two ladies to the door. Mallory slipped into the cab and shut and locked the doors. Her head fell back on the seat and she let loose the anguish that filled her body and her soul.

For a few short and glorious weeks, she'd basked in the confidence of being cherished by someone who wanted nothing from her except what she was willing to give. Now, brick by mental brick, mile by mile, as the cab made the long trip across the water and through the tunnel to Virginia Beach, Mallory reconstructed the wall that had been her refuge all these years.

That night, not even Consuela, who had been waiting in case she needed something, could console her. Her bed, normally a refuge, reminded her of the love she'd made there with Ellis.

"That two-timing, double-crossing snake."

Mallory fell across the bed in one of her two guest suites. She cried herself to sleep, cursing herself for the gullible fool she'd been in learning to trust and to love Ellis Carson.

At Jeanette's apartment in Newport News, Ellis fumed. "What did you say to her?"

"Nothing," the pregnant woman said, from her propped up position on the sofa. "She introduced herself as Mallory Heart. I asked her if she was one of the people from the Heart Department Stores. She said yes and then she went tearing out of the hospital like a bat was after her."

"She asked about the baby," a small voice said.

Ellis and Jeanette turned toward the voice. "What are you doing up, precious? You're supposed to be asleep."

"I'm worried about Ray-Ray," Quandra said. "He looked like he was still in pain."

Jeanette cast anxious eyes at Ellis.

"I'll check on him." Ellis got up from the chair where he'd been questioning Jeanette and went to check on the toddler. A few minutes later, he came back. "He's fine, Quan."

The girl didn't look convinced, though. "Maybe I'll sit in a chair by his bed."

"Quandra, that's not . . ." Jeanette began. But Ellis silenced her with a small wave.

"If that'll make you feel better, you do that, okay?" he told the girl.

She nodded and disappeared back down the hall.

"She blames herself," Ellis explained.

Jeanette sighed as she shifted her position on the sofa.

"I told her it wasn't her fault that he got sick. Mallory told her, too. She was really good with them this evening," he said, a small smile curving his mouth.

Jeanette watched him, then sighed again. "She's the one y'all were talking about that day, the woman you're in love with."

Ellis looked at Jeanette. "I can't believe it myself," he said. "But, yeah. We're like from two different worlds, forbidden worlds, and yet . . ." He shook his head.

Jeanette bit her lip. "I think I know why she left without saying anything to you."

"Why? What happened?"

"Well, I didn't mean it to come out the way it did, but I think she thinks you're the baby's father. That we're, like, you know, a couple."

Ellis frowned. "Now how in the world would she get a crazy idea like that?"

"Gee, thanks, Ellis. And here I was all ready to name the baby after you."

That made him pause. "You were?"

Jeanette nodded. "The kids and I took a vote on

names. It was unanimous. You've done so much for us. We wanted to say thanks, but didn't know how until we started talking about names for the baby."

He grinned. "That's pretty cool." Then he frowned. "And what is Dexter G. gonna think about his kid being named after me?"

Jeanette leaned back and plucked a long white envelope from the end table. She handed the letter to Ellis. "He thinks it's a great idea."

Ellis, accepting the envelope, looked at the return address and the Newport News Jail stamp on the backside of it.

"Go ahead," Jeanette said. "Read it."

Opening the envelope, Ellis read the three-page letter. In it, Dexter Grantwood, Jeanette's boyfriend, talked about how grateful he was that a righteous brother was looking after her and the kids while he did his time. He'd committed his life to Christ while behind bars and told Jeanette about how things would be when he was released in another four months.

Ellis nodded as he finished reading the letter. "That's good, Jeanette. That's real good for you and the kids."

"Twan and Quandra's father sent me some money for them. The check arrived the other day. It was a money order, too. So I know it's good."

Steepling his hands in front of him, Ellis nodded. He didn't mention that he'd seen to that detail, or that he'd found Jeanette's ex-husband and threatened to do him some serious harm if he didn't start taking care of his responsibilities.

"What about Antwan and Dexter?"

"Dexter's been sending him a letter every now and then, too. Telling him that he's glad I have him here, that he's looking forward to being a father figure for him."

"And what'd Twan say to that?"

Jeanette looked away.

"Come on, tell me," Ellis urged.

"He's still mad at his dad for leaving," she said.

"And?"

"And he's mad at you for leaving."

"I haven't gone anywhere."

"But you will," she said. "His father left him. When Dex gets out, I know you'll probably stop spending so much time over here. So Twan is, well, he's just being Twan."

"I'll have a talk with him, okay?"

Jeanette nodded. "It's getting kind of late, Ellis. You better check on your ladyfriend. I think she's pretty upset."

The thought of Mallory reminded Ellis of his personal priorities. He got up, kissed Jeanette on the cheek, then went to check on the kids before leaving.

He thought about everything that had transpired so far with Mallory as he drove home. She either wasn't picking up the phone or was screening her calls. It was too late to go knocking on her door right now.

"In the morning though, Miss Mallory, we're gonna have a little talk," he promised himself. He was serious about her and wanted to know just where their relationship was going to go. He had definite plans, permanent ones that included her in them.

Chapter 14

Mallory had her own plans. The light of day and the circles under her eyes gave testimony to the night she'd had. But it was a new day. And the Mallory who kicked butt and took names was back—with a vengeance.

At Mallory's Place, she drank her water, ate a muffin, and perused the newspaper. But her thoughts kept returning to Ellis Carson's treachery.

"Played like a fool," she said.

Mallory, however, had been playing hardball her entire life. People like her cousin Cole and her Aunt Virginia had honed her skills. She mentally reviewed every lie she'd been told by Ellis. As she was running down the list, her eye caught a small headline on the business page: *Knight & Kraus Begins Bid Process.*

A memory flashed through her mind. It took less than a second for it to come back. Ellis had gotten mail from Knight & Kraus. Suddenly, all of the pieces fell into place. Ellis's company wasn't applying for credit with Knight & Kraus. He hoped to build those stores that had ruined her.

Mallory cursed herself a double fool.

"You trusted him!" she wailed in her office. "You trusted him."

She paced the area, thinking, wondering, plotting. He'd made a fool of her. Well, she could play the game and hit him where it really hurt.

Snatching up the phone, Mallory cradled it in the recess between her ear and shoulder while she flipped through her Rolodex. Yanking a card from the file, she quickly dialed the number, then sat down as the line rang.

A smile crossed her face and she leaned back. She'd show Ellis Carson just who had the upper hand.

"Hi, Walter. It's Mallory. Mallory Heart. How have you been?"

She settled back in her chair. Walter Jemison owed her a favor—several in fact. Mallory was calling in a chip with the man who could make bids disappear and questions arise about otherwise pristine business reputations.

* * *

That afternoon, Mallory was interviewing salesclerks when she felt him enter the store. That her awareness of Ellis was so keen didn't sit well with her. She'd ignored his calls and didn't return his messages.

She completed the review of the application of the young woman before her, then handed the woman a plastic key with three notches on it. "Take this to the area over there. My assistant will show you what to do next."

"Hey, Mallory."

She kept her attention on the roster of names she was reviewing. The last candidate was a good one. If she passed the last customer service tryout, she'd be in.

"Mallory."

Not even glancing at him, she got up and went to her office.

Ellis followed. When she tried to shut the door in his face, he lost his patience.

"You've been playing the wounded role for long enough, Mallory. You tried and convicted me without taking into consideration any of the evidence."

"Evidence? I saw the evidence all right. It looks due with your baby any day now."

Ellis shook his head. "This would be funny if I were in the mood for games. But I've got to get back to the office. Something's come up with a bid we put in for some work."

Mallory smiled. "Oh, really? That's too bad. Maybe the next department store that rolls into town will be more amenable to the work you do."

Ellis's eyes narrowed. "What are you talking about? And how'd you know I was talking about a department store bid?"

She sauntered to her desk and slowly took a seat. This victory felt good. Knight & Kraus had wrecked her professional world. Ellis Carson had wrecked her emotional world. Confident that Walter Jemison's magic was already working, she crossed her legs and swiveled slowly in the chair.

"Just a wild guess."

Something in her countenance, the smugness, the surety, tipped him off. A chill ran down Ellis's back. "What did you do, Mallory?"

Leaning back, she looked up at him glowering at her from across her expansive Italian desk. "I gave as I got," she said. "Feels good, too."

Ellis rounded the desk and grabbed her arms, yanking her up. "What did you do?"

"Let go of me," she said, twisting away from him. She rubbed her arms where he'd grabbed her. "I bet you don't manhandle your little girlfriend like that."

"She's not my girlfriend." The words, clipped and angry, seemed forced from his mouth.

Mallory blanched. "Oh, my God. You slept with me when your wife was home pregnant with your son."

She lifted her chin, meeting his icy glare. Carelessly plunging on, she tried to hurt him as much as he'd hurt her. "Well, thanks for the sex lesson, Ellis. Now that I know the basics, maybe I'll go find someone who shows a little technique."

Ellis stood before her, too angry to speak, afraid that what he wanted to do to her right now could actually manifest itself in physical violence. "I don't know what you're talking about," he said slowly, carefully. "As a matter of fact, I don't think you know, either. But since you're hell bent on believing what you want to believe, go with it."

She smiled. "I plan to."

A tick flicked at the corner of his eye. They stared at each other for a long time. Mallory was good at that game though. In her day she'd intimidated greater men than Ellis Carson.

When she was sure she had the upper hand in the standoff, she delivered the death blow. "I wouldn't count on that Knight & Kraus project if I were you," she said.

She sat down and folded her hands on the desk. "Your check will be in the mail for the work your outfit did here. Our business is done, Mr. Carson. Good day."

Then, picking up a piece of paper and studying it, she dismissed him like a peon.

A moment later, the door slammed. Glass shattered all around as the imported stained glass in her office door gave way under the force. Mallory stared at the damage, wondering why the thrill of victory hadn't descended on her yet.

Three weeks later, Mallory's Place looked like the upscale boutique it was meant to be. Along with the assistant manager and three sales clerks she'd hired, Mallory was stocking the shop, arranging displays, and putting in the final touches.

The official grand opening of the store was another few weeks away, but Mallory decided to quietly open for business just as soon as possible. She'd been unable to do much else in the days since the showdown with Ellis.

She'd replaced the stained glass he'd broken on his way out and had hired all of the staff. She'd cut the check for the work Ellis's Quality Construction Company had done and had had lunch with Walter Jemison, who'd assured her that Quality Construction's chances of getting the Knight & Kraus project were slim to none.

But Mallory found no victory in knowing she'd wielded the power to crush him. Instead, she'd lost about ten pounds and had perpetual circles under her eyes from not being able to sleep.

"Should the belts go here or over there?" Irene, the assistant manager asked.

"It doesn't matter," Mallory said. "I'm going to take a break. I'll be in the office."

"Is everything all right?"

Mallory nodded. "Yes, everything's fine. The store looks great. You've done a marvelous job."

The woman beamed under the praise but was obviously concerned about her employer. "Can I get you some tea, maybe some Evian?"

Shaking her head as she walked, Mallory reached the office then closed the door behind her. She sank into the Louis XV chair in front of the desk and wondered if she should call the Heart family therapist for some antidepressants. She'd been in a funk for weeks now.

Her dream, her vision, was finally a reality. And she didn't care.

"Not one bit," she said out loud. She slumped in the chair and stared at the small Picasso on her wall. The painting had been a gift from a congressman she'd dated once. Looking at it made Mallory realize that she and Ellis had never exchanged gifts or mementos.

All he'd left her with were memories of tender lovemaking and, now, regrets.

For a long time, she just sat there, feeling sorry for herself and sorry about what she'd done to Ellis. A knock on the door broke into her melancholy.

"Come in."

Irene stepped into the office. "There's a gentleman here to see you," she said.

Expecting Ellis, Mallory jumped up. But it wasn't Ellis who came into the office. Bailey walked in wearing jeans, work boots, and a Quality Construction T-shirt.

"Hello, Ms. Heart," he said.

Mallory's face lit up. "Hi, Bailey. Come on in. What brings you here?"

Irene slipped out. Mallory offered Bailey a chair, but he declined. He reached into his T-shirt pocket and pulled out a piece of paper.

"I'm not here long, Ms. Heart. I just came to give you this." He handed the folded-over paper to her.

Mallory opened it then turned confused eyes to him. "I don't understand," she said. "Why are you returning my check? Your company did all of the work. You even did it in less time than you'd originally estimated."

Bailey cleared his throat. "We don't want your money, Ms. Heart. Ellis would have just sent it back in the mail, but I told him I'd bring the check back."

"I don't understand."

"No, I guess you wouldn't," he said. He folded his big arms and stared at her. "Ellis believes in doing right by people, even when they do him wrong. That's something he learned a long time ago. You put the fix in so we weren't in the running for the mall project. Ellis sweated a lot of hours putting that bid together. We would have been contenders. I know that to be true."

Mallory had the grace to look embarrassed. "He lied to me."

"And to pay him back, you took food off the tables and clothes off the backs of hard-working men and women."

She blanched.

"But don't you worry about that, Ms. Heart. Carson Quality Contracting is still a viable company. No thanks to you."

There was something Mallory needed to know. "Did his wife or girlfriend, or whoever she is, have the baby?"

Bailey nodded. "Jeanette and the baby are doing just fine. She was even able to take him to visit his father."

A whisper of dread floated through Mallory's mind. "What do you mean, 'took him to visit his father'? Where's Ellis?"

"Oh, Ellis is in town—at his house—although these days he's been spending a lot more time at the office. He's been writing bids; not projects as big as the mall department stores. For some reason, we seem to be blacklisted. But you wouldn't know anything about that, would you?"

Mallory became more uncomfortable by the minute as her dismay grew. "I, I . . ." When she tried to speak, her voice wavered. Something had gone horribly wrong.

She slumped into her desk chair and stared up at Bailey. His Southern charm had been replaced by a steely look that was probably reserved for child molesters and wife abusers. She did an assessment and realized she didn't know a few crucial details.

"Bailey, would you please tell me something?"

"What you want to know, Ms. Heart?"

"What is Jeanette to Ellis?"

He chuckled without mirth then shuffled his feet. "Why do you want to know now? Seems like you've already come to all the necessary conclusions."

Mallory wanted to snap at him to stop the Gomer Pyle routine and just answer the question. But she didn't. Her anger had already done damage that could very well be irreparable. She needed to know the truth, and if it didn't come from Ellis's mouth, Bailey's was the next best thing.

"Please," she said.

For a long, tense moment, Bailey studied her. Then, apparently making up his mind, he exhaled. "Ellis met Jeanette when she signed her son, Antwan, up to get a Big Brother."

Mallory closed her eyes. It was worse than she'd thought.

"Her husband walked out on her and their two kids, leaving her with essentially just the clothes on their backs. He'd hocked everything of value and left her with a trail of bad credit. She went on welfare, moved into the projects, and tried to make the best of her situation."

"Ellis isn't the father of her baby, is he?"

"No. Carson doesn't have any kids, except for the ones he's adopted as a Big Brother or a confidant."

Mallory's sigh held the weight of the world in it. She'd been wrong—so horribly wrong.

"Ellis and Antwan clicked from the moment they met. When Jeanette started dating an activist named Dexter, Ellis pulled back. He didn't want to create conflict in the relationship. But, then, Dexter was arrested."

"What did he do?"

"Hit a cop."

Mallory pursed her lips at that.

"There's a lot more to it," Bailey said. "But it's not really relevant to what you want to know."

She cast brown eyes up at him. "He thinks I'm awful, doesn't he?"

"That and a few other things."

"I'm sorry," she said.

Bailey shrugged. "I'm not the one you need to be apologizing to. I'm just the bearer of the check."

She picked it up. "Why are you returning the money? The company earned it."

Bailey shook his head. "Carson wants no part of vengeful money."

She opened her mouth to protest, then closed it, realizing the argument wasn't one to have with Bailey. She dropped the check on the desk and stood up. "Thank you for coming over, Bailey. I'm glad you did."

He watched her. "What are you gonna do now?"

She shrugged. "What can I do? I don't think he's going to take my calls. If I sent a letter, he wouldn't read it. What's the point?"

"Well, I heard Big Mama say something one time, and I'll pass it along to you."

"What's that?"

"Love will find a way."

Chapter 15

Ellis tugged on the stiff collar of his dress shirt. The tie was new. So was the suit. He longed for a pair of comfortable jeans and a T-shirt, but that attire wasn't suitable for court. He'd been served a summons to appear as a witness. Try as he might, he couldn't seem to get a straight answer out of anybody in the clerk's office about just what or who he was supposed to be a witness to.

No one was in the courtroom, but he'd been assured by a bailiff that he was in the right place. Just about the time he was getting ready to leave, a door opened and in walked two deputies. Mallory walked between them, her head bowed. She was dressed in . . . It looked like an orange jail jumpsuit!

"What the hell?" he muttered.

Spectators filed in, including Sheila from the office and some of his crew. When Jeanette wheeled the baby's carriage into the courtroom, Ellis stood up. Bailey walked in another door and took a seat next to Ellis, pulling him down as he sat.

"What the devil is going on here?" Ellis demanded.

"Mallory's on trial," Bailey said.

"On trial for what?"

"Shh," a bailiff demanded.

"All rise. The Honorable Rufus H. Smith is presiding." Ellis stood along with the other people in the courtroom as a black-robed judge entered the courtroom.

Looking confused, Ellis sat when the others did.

"Will the defendant face the court," the judge said.

Mallory rose and walked to the area facing the judge. A deputy swore her in.

"Mallory Elaine Heart, you stand accused of jumping to conclusions, making false accusations, and being a menace to society. How do you plead?"

"What is this?" Ellis said, jumping up. Bailey bit back a smile.

"Order in the court," the judge said, with a scowl in Ellis's direction.

Ellis rolled his eyes and sat down.

"I plead guilty, Your Honor," Mallory said.

She turned and faced the gallery. "I wronged some innocent people," she said. "I harmed the reputations of people who didn't deserve to be wronged. And I hurt the person who, I've discovered, means the world to me."

An eyebrow rose on Ellis's otherwise placid face.

"To Ms. Jeanette Kent, I'm sorry for treating you badly," Mallory said.

"To Bailey, I apologize for taking my anger out on you. And to all of the crew at Carson Quality Contracting, I'm sorry for being such a royal pain in the you-know-what during the time you were working on my shop."

"Is that all you have to say for yourself?" the judge asked.

Mallory turned to face him, then shook her head. "No, Your Honor. There's someone else."

The judge waved a hand. "Well, get on with it. We don't have all night."

Mallory faced the gallery again and walked toward Ellis. She paused when the only thing that separated them was a wooden railing.

"I'm on trial today because what I did to you was criminal," she said.

He folded his arms and glared at her. Bailey nudged him in the side. Ellis frowned and looked straight ahead, ignoring Mallory.

"About three months ago, I met a man who changed my world," Mallory said. "He challenged me. He provoked me. He made me see that the way I lived my life wasn't, well, it wasn't perfect. He introduced me to people and to situations that I never would have encountered. I fell in love with him," she said.

Ellis's gaze flicked over her, sharp and assessing. He unfolded his arms, a small sign that encouraged Mallory.

"All my life, people have jumped to do my bidding. This man not only refused to jump, he made me realize that I couldn't treat people like resources designed to make my own life easier."

"And what happened?" the judge asked.

"I returned what he freely gave me with vengeance. There's nothing I can do to right that particular wrong, but I have made restitution in other ways."

Ellis folded his arms and crossed one leg over his knee.

"What did you do?" the judge asked.

Mallory swallowed. This was all she had. If Ellis couldn't forgive her and see that she'd learned a valuable life lesson, she didn't know what she'd do.

"Ms. Heart?" the judge prompted.

She blinked. And then, with her full attention on Ellis, she began. "Your Honor, to make restitution to Ms. Jeanette Kent and her children, I established a college fund for Antwan and Quandra Kent. For their stepbrothers, Ray-Ray and Ellis Grantwood, I've done the same plus made a contribution to the local Sickle

Cell Anemia association in Ray-Ray Grantwood's name. For the children in their neighborhood, I've ordered playground equipment and landscaping services."

"Isn't that a public housing project?"

"Yes, sir. I've gotten all the necessary approvals and permits from the city."

The judge nodded. "That all?"

Mallory bowed her head. "I've committed to three hundred hours of community service in low-income neighborhoods, sir. That's all I could do with money and time, Your Honor. For the rest, I'm throwing myself on the mercy of the court."

"Hmmm," the judge said. He glanced at a piece of paper. "Okay. I'm going to call a witness on your behalf. I understand just one has been subpoenaed. "Ellis Carson, approach the bench."

Ellis frowned. Bailey nudged him and he stood up. He walked past Mallory.

"Nice outfit," he said.

For the first time, Mallory smiled.

A deputy swore Ellis in. "You know, I get the feeling this isn't a real court of law," he muttered.

The stony-faced deputy didn't crack a smile. Ellis faced the judge.

"Ellis Carson, you're the sole remaining injured party in this case, according to the file. Would you care to state your grievance?"

Ellis turned and looked at Mallory. She seemed thinner . . . and wiser. She was still, however, as beautiful as she'd been the first day they met. His gaze flicked over the orange jumpsuit that covered her body, hiding from his view the legs he liked so much.

Turning back to the judge, Ellis shook his head. "No, sir. I think Ms. Heart outlined her case very well."

"Hmmm," the judge said, with a glance in Mallory's direction. "Well," he said, clearing his throat. "That being the case, I have two questions for you, Mr. Carson."

"Shoot," Ellis said.

The judge scowled at him.

"Sorry," Ellis mumbled.

"I want you to take your time answering them both, Mr. Carson. Your responses are very important. Do you understand?"

Ellis nodded.

"Well, then. The first question: Can you forgive Ms. Mallory Heart for what she did against you?"

Ellis glanced back at Mallory, then his gaze wandered over the other people in the courtroom. Ned, the crew chief who'd been in charge of Mallory's work was there. So were the men who'd worked on Mallory's store. He figured a group of women he didn't recognize were probably Mallory's friends or employees.

Jeanette grinned at him and nodded. He looked to her left and saw Big Mama sitting there. For the first time, he couldn't read her expression. It was as though she were telling him he was on his own with this.

"Oh, man. I don't believe this," Ellis muttered.

"What was that, Mr. Carson? I didn't hear you."

Ellis ran a hand over his face. "Nothing, Your Honor."

"Well? What's your answer?"

He looked at Mallory again. She seemed as if she were holding her breath.

Facing the judge, Ellis stood straight and tall. "Yes, Your Honor. I can forgive Mallory Heart."

An audible sigh rippled through the courtroom, and conversation went up.

"Hush up," the judge said. "We're not done here."

When the courtroom quieted down again, the judge commanded Ellis's attention. "You have another question to answer, young man."

Ellis clasped his hands in front of him, waiting. The judge looked first at Mallory, who, other than Ellis, was the only person standing in the room, then he turned his full attention back to Ellis.

"My final question to you is this, Mr. Carson. Do you love Mallory Heart?"

A feather falling would have made the sound of a cannon in the suddenly still courtroom. Ellis stared at the judge for a long time. Then he turned and looked at Mallory. He faced the judge again.

"May I approach the bench, or whatever it is lawyers say when they want to step up?"

The judge scowled. "Yes."

Ellis came forward and motioned for the judge to lean closer. He whispered something. The judge looked up once, frowned, and then put his ear back to Ellis. After a moment, the judge straightened. So did Ellis.

"The court would ask Ms. Mallory Heart to approach the bench."

Mallory started as though someone poked a pin in her side. She then quickly made her way up front, where she stood next to Ellis. She glanced at him, but he didn't meet her look.

"Ten minute recess," the judge announced. Then to Mallory and Ellis, "You two, in my chambers."

Ellis and Mallory followed the judge.

In chambers, Ellis turned and faced Mallory. "What are you doing?"

She glanced at the judge, who ignored them both as he went to pour a cup of coffee. "Trying to make you understand just how sorry I am about everything. I acted out of anger and I should know better."

"Why'd you sabotage my bid?"

Mallory swallowed. "Do you mind if I sit?"

Ellis held a hand out toward one of the leather chairs in the judge's chamber. She sank into it and clasped her hands together. "I decided to launch Mallory's Place after I was booted from Knight & Kraus," she said.

"What? I thought you worked for your family's department stores."

"I did," Mallory said. "All my life I've been in competition with a cousin who ended up with the CEO spot that should have been mine. To get even, I brokered a buy-out deal. The stores were in trouble anyway. The buy out would give all of the family shareholders lots of money, and it would breathe new life into the stores. Selling to Knight & Kraus meant giving up the Heart name, though. They would turn our Virginia and North Carolina stores into Knight & Kraus department stores and then venture into all of the local malls."

"That's where I came in," Ellis said.

She nodded. "At your office one day, I saw an envelope with their logo and address on it. I put two and two together and saw red."

"So why don't you work for them?"

"For brokering the deal, I was to get a vice presidency in Knight & Kraus and a significant signing bonus for making the deal happen."

"But?"

"But they looked at my cousin's track record and offered him the job."

Ellis whistled. "Screwed again, huh?"

Mallory nodded. "So I left. I took my own money and decided to start Mallory's Place."

"And this cousin of yours, he's in charge at the company now?"

Mallory laughed, the sound bitter. "He told them to go to hell. He married a consultant he'd been working with to save the stores. I haven't seen or talked to him since and don't care to."

"That's not a healthy attitude, Mallory," the judge said. "Cole has had just as hard a time of things as you have."

"And who is Cole?"

Mallory scowled. "My cousin. By the way, this is my Uncle Rufus," she said, introducing the two men, "retired Judge Rufus Heart Smith, one of the few relatives I actually get along with. This is Ellis Carson."

Ellis laughed. "Man, you people with money can pull all sorts of strings, can't you? What'd it cost to get this courtroom?"

Mallory reached for his hand. "It's not about money, Ellis. It's about heart," she said, touching her own heart. "Out there, you said you could forgive me. The second question, about whether or not you loved me, is one that, well, was probably presumptuous of me."

When he didn't say or do anything, Mallory's hand dropped away. "No matter how you feel about me," she said, "I want you to know that I love you very much. You opened my eyes and my heart, and for that I'm forever grateful."

In the face of his continued silence, Mallory sighed. Her uncle offered a small shrug, meant as condolence. Mallory rubbed her hands together, then unfastened the orange jail jumpsuit. She stepped out of the jail issue shoes and straightened the fire-engine-red of her short suit skirt. She reached for her own high-heeled mules and slipped them on.

"Thanks for your time, Uncle Rufus. I know you have a dinner engagement."

The judge nodded and then patted Mallory's hand. With a final look at Ellis, Mallory picked up a small handbag from the judge's desk and turned to leave.

He let her get all the way to the door.

"Mallory."

She turned, hopeful, but knowing she'd live a long time regretting her actions against Ellis.

"Did I ever tell you that you have the best-looking legs I've ever seen on a woman?"

She smiled. "Thank you." The compliment was nice, but it wasn't what she'd hoped to hear from him. She reached for the door knob.

"Hey, Mallory."

Facing him, she turned. "Yes, Ellis?"

"If I tell you that I love you, are you going to hold that against me for the rest of my life?"

A smile started at her mouth and crept up until her entire face beamed. "Only if you want me to."

Ellis covered the distance between them. "I do."

"I want to be clear on this, Ellis. I need to understand completely what you're saying."

"I'm saying I love you, woman. What else does a man have to say?"

She threw her arms around his neck. "Nothing. Not one thing."

When they came together, the kiss was apology and renewal. She curled into his body, and his hands roamed over her back and slid lower. She needed more of him and his eager mouth told her the same was true of him.

Mallory, filled with a sense of joy and rightness, rained kisses on him.

The judge cleared his throat when the two seemed as though they were going to take the embrace to another level—one that needed to be private.

Ellis lifted his head from the exploration of Mallory's neck. "Yes, Your Honor?"

"This case is closed. Court adjourned."

Ellis grinned. Then he turned his attention back to the woman who'd opened his heart, aroused his senses, and promised to love him as much as he loved her.

If you enjoyed Mallory Heart's story, be sure to read the beginning of the Heart saga. In **FOOLISH HEART,** Mallory's cousin Coleman learns that appearances and motivations can be deceiving. Here's an excerpt from Cole Heart and Sonja Pride's love story.

FOOLISH HEART
By Felicia Mason

ISBN 0-7860-0593-9

Prologue

Twenty years was a long time to wait for justice, but, finally, the day had come. Coleman Heart would be sorry he ever tangled with the Pride family.

Sonja Pride would be victorious and her struggle more than worth the wait when the entire Heart family, in particular Cole Heart, found itself bankrupt or floundering. She wanted to see them insolvent and humiliated, just the way they'd left so many others.

She'd built up her own business the old-fashioned way—with hard work and sleepless nights. Her entire career had been painstakingly calculated for this moment, the final act in a play that began long before Sonja knew words like *revenge, retribution* and *retaliate,* long before she'd tasted defeat and poverty.

"Payback is a mother," she said.

Sonja smiled and lifted a crystal champagne glass. The light amber liquid sparkled like the determination in her eyes.

Tonight she toasted perseverance.

Soon, she'd toast sweet vengeance.

Chapter 1

Sonja Pride's heels clicked smartly on the black marble foyer leading to the offices of Coleman Heart III. For their eight-thirty appointment, she'd arrived forty-five minutes early. She needed the extra time for the pep talk she always gave herself before meeting with a client.

And this client was special; so special that Sonja had to force herself to remember her role, to remember the cause and the plan.

She'd never met Coleman Heart III, but she had his arrogant image indelibly stamped in her memory. The research her people had done for this job was extraordinary; the results of their investigation damning. Coleman Heart's employees were robbing him blind, and he didn't even know it.

The news buoyed her already high spirits, and her smile broadened.

"Good morning."

She glanced at the man who held a glass door open for her and marked him for what he was—a Heart. He had the look—the square jaw, strong chin, and thick lashes all the males seemed to favor. This one was young, maybe in his early twenties.

She smiled at him. "Hello."

"I hope you're going my way."

"Not unless you're Coleman Heart III," she told him.

"Cole has all the luck. I'm heading to his office for a meeting, though. Follow me."

"Good morning," he called to a receptionist at the front desk.

"Good morning, Mr. Heart. Cole is waiting for you."

The younger Heart grimaced. "He's here at the crack of dawn every day. I don't think he sleeps."

"They say the early bird catches the worm," Sonja replied as she fell into step beside him.

"My uncle is here *before* the worms."

Ah, Sonja thought as her mental checklist clicked in. *This would be the nephew, Lance.* Brown educated,

Coleman's favorite, perceived to be the heir-in-training.

Sonja glanced at the cute kid and ratcheted his age up to about twenty-five. He seemed friendly enough, was probably even a nice guy. Too bad her job was to make sure he had nothing to inherit from his long line of reprobate relatives.

She couldn't let herself get distracted by that part of the mission. Not yet.

They turned left and walked a wide, curving hallway. This was where the money lived. The carpeting was deep and luxurious. Windows outlined some of the offices in the outer circle, while an eclectic mix of art work graced the inner walls. Sonja recognized a Henry O. Tanner painting and a Varnette P. Honeywood. She spied expensive looking antiques through the open doors of one office. To the right, the wall gave way to a glass-enclosed conference room, probably where the board members met.

They passed four doors on the left before the nephew paused.

"Let me grab my pad," he said. He dashed into a smaller office and was right back with a leather portfolio.

"Right this way. My office is next to Cole's. I didn't get your name," he said.

"Sonja Pride. From The Pride Group."

The young man took her hand and pumped it. His infectious grin made Sonja smile.

"I'm Lance Heart Smith, and we've been waiting for you. Come right on in."

They passed through a small but efficient office, then into the larger one.

The first thing Sonja noticed when she stepped into Coleman Heart's private space was the absence of pretension. The simplicity hit her like a fist. After the opulence and indulgence of the inner circle and the palatial looks of some of the offices, this seemed, well, downright ordinary for a CEO. A single watercolor, a painting of either dawn or sunset, she couldn't tell which, graced the wall. A few healthy green plants were scattered about. File cabinets in a dark wood hid papers and clutter. The focal point of the room was clearly the large desk, made of cherry or some other hard wood. A PC and a smaller monitor were there, as were a telephone and neat stacks of paperwork. A comfortable looking conversation group was on one side of the room, a round conference table on the other.

This room looked as if someone actually did real work in it. While large, it was an office, not a playground for a man who kept a seat warm while collecting a paycheck and capital gains he didn't earn.

"Have a seat," Lance invited. "I'll get Cole."

Before he could turn toward the door, Cole Heart burst through it with a harried looking woman in his wake. She ripped plastic from a bag of dry cleaning as he buttoned his white shirt with one hand and yelled at someone on a cell phone in the other.

"Sell, dammit. I don't care what your recommendation is."

"Mason, get me on a plane to Aspen this weekend. I need to relax before heading to Detroit," he said.

"No, I do not want Pistons tickets," he told the person on the phone. "Just handle the stock." He snapped the phone shut and tossed it to the woman, who traded him his suit jacket for the telephone. He shrugged into the double-breasted, gray pinstripe.

"Where do you want to stay?" the woman asked.

"The usual. And make sure the car isn't a toy this time. I need space."

"I'm sorry," she said as she handed him a tie. "I thought that reservation was for—"

They both abruptly halted when they spied Lance and Sonja.

Cole looked as if he wanted to let out an expletive. The woman darted frantic eyes to her empty desk in the anteroom.

Cole took the situation under control. He strode to Sonja in bold steps and stuck out a large, strong hand.

"Good morning. You must be Sonja Pride. You're early. I like that."

Overpowering.

And god-awful sexy.

She'd seen photographs of him, usually mug shots

that accompanied newspaper stories. Nothing in her experience or expectations had prepared her for this. He stood at least six-foot-three, with broad shoulders that tapered to a narrow waist. His eyes were a dark gray. *Contacts?* she wondered. Whatever, the entire package was a presence to be reckoned with.

It took Sonja a moment to get her scattered thoughts together. She had the advantage here, and needed to capitalize on it.

"Hello," she said.

Shaking his hand, she had to admit that everything about this man seemed larger than life. Did he eat innocent virgins for breakfast?

"Why don't you finish dressing?" She glanced at the round conference table on the other side of his desk. "I'll just set up over there. Is that all right?"

"That will be fine."

He glared at Lance, and then the hostile expression was gone. "Mason. Coffee, please."

"Yes, sir."

Moments later, fully dressed and buttoned down, Cole was at Sonja's side.

"Let's start again," he said. "I'm Cole Heart. It looks as if you've already met Lance Heart Smith." He paused with a stern look in Lance's direction, then added, "My intern."

"I'm really an executive assistant." But Lance's nervous chuckle told the story about what might be his rapidly diminishing status.

Sonja nodded. "Well, it's a pleasure to meet you both. May I plug this somewhere?" She held up a cord attached to a compact laptop.

Lance jumped to do her bidding. "Right here," he said as he pressed a small groove in the middle of the table. An electrical socket popped up.

"Excellent."

Mason, Cole's assistant, brought in coffee and muffins, placed them within reach on the table, then disappeared.

Cole indicated a chair for Sonja. "Well," he said, taking his own seat, "what news do you have?"

Sonja indicated the spiral-bound reports she'd placed on the table. Handing one to Cole and then one to Lance, she powered the computer. "Well, as the saying goes, I have good news and bad news."

Cole glanced at Lance, who hovered near the computer. "Is that a WinBook XLi?" the young man asked.

"Yes," Sonja said with a smile. "Top of the line. It's wonderful."

"I've been thinking about getting one of those. Is the CD-Rom drive built in?"

"Lance."

Cole's tone said, *One more distraction or screwup, and you're outta here.*

Chagrined, Lance sat and opened the report from Sonja, who indicated the laptop and nodded at him.

"Give me the bad first," Cole said.

"Well, it's not that easy," Sonja said. "Let's just start at the beginning."

Nodding his acquiescence, Cole sat back. Lance eyed the laptop.

"When you contracted with The Pride Group, you asked that we shop your stores for the total shopping experience from a customer's perspective. Over the course of two weeks, a team of eleven people worked your stores. Five shopped the three stores here in Virginia. We sent two shoppers to work the three stores in North Carolina. Another four floated among all of the stores. We wanted to give you as broad a perspective as possible from several shopping experiences."

"I asked that someone pose as an employee, as well," Cole interjected.

Sonja nodded and pressed a key to begin the Powerpoint presentation on the computer. "Yes, we did that too, focusing as you asked on the flagship store in Hampton and the one in the Virginia Beach area."

"And?"

She glanced at him and decided he didn't need to be spared any details. But, oh, how she wanted to drag out the pain.

"On page three of the report, you'll see the classifications."

Lance turned to the indicated page.

Cole simply stared at Sonja until she cleared her throat.

"Heart Federated Stores gets high marks for store design and floor layout. There's a logical, customer-oriented flow in each store."

"Aunt Justine will be glad to hear that, huh Cole?" Lance said. "She did all the decorating and layout," he added for Sonja's benefit.

A quelling look from Cole silenced Lance.

"Sorry," the young man murmured. He dropped his gaze back to his report.

"What's the *but,* Ms. Pride?" Cole asked.

"The *'but,'* Mr. Heart, is that the most important asset in each of the six stores we surveyed is downplayed, sometimes outright ignored."

"And that asset would be?"

"Your customers, Mr. Heart."

His frown should have discouraged her, but Sonja sat there practically giddy. Tamping down her glee and maintaining her professional decorum, Sonja continued.

"It's well documented that businesses with mediocre product but excellent customer service fare better than those with excellent products and dismal customer care. Of course, the ideal is a business atmosphere—in this case a shopping experience—that rates high marks for the quality of its products as well as its care of the customer and his satisfaction."

"How did Heart stores rate in your survey?"

"Not very well, Cole, according to this," Lance said.

Sonja's finger glided over the touchpad and two

pie charts flowed onto the monitor. "On the left in green are comparable stores. On the right in blue is Heart Federated."

Cole looked at the illustration and frowned. The scowl he sent Sonja's way would have intimidated a less focused woman.

"You're telling me that customers hate everything about Heart stores?"

"Not everything. Just the way they're treated by the sales staff," she said.

"That *is* everything."

Sonja nodded. "We got the impression that there is little or no customer service or customer retention training at any of the stores."

"But what about the orientation program?" Lance asked. "That's where they're supposed to get trained. It's twenty-five hours the first week of employment, and twenty-five hours during the second week."

For once, Cole didn't scowl at Lance. He nodded in his nephew's direction then looked to Sonja for confirmation.

"The Pride Group employee assigned to the Virginia Beach store was hired there four weeks ago. Each of his scheduled training sessions has been postponed because the department manager was short-staffed on the floor. At the Hampton store, our representative was told—" Sonja consulted her notes and then read verbatim, " 'That orientation stuff isn't really important. All you need to know is how to SKU and how to run the register.' She's been there three weeks. Both employees said they did receive an hour of special training on spotting counterfeit currency. And both reported that during a lunchbreak in the employee lounge, a video on diversity awareness was playing on a continuous-loop tape. The Virginia Beach employee said the sound was muted on the VCR."

Sonja continued with her presentation, citing concrete examples and anecdotal evidence of the poor state of the Heart Department Stores. From salesclerks with attitudes to dirty rest rooms, she covered it all. By the time she finished, thunder and lightning marched across Cole's features.

"Mr. Heart, there's something else you need to know." She glanced at Lance, not sure how much to say in front of him.

"What is it?" he barked. "Lance is family."

"Employee theft is at just about thirty percent."

The explosion came, swift and sure.

"I don't know what kind of games you're playing here, Ms. Pride. I brought you in on the recommendation of a board member who thought you did good work. Don't you think I'd know if my own people were stealing from me?"

"Maybe, maybe not," she said. "I thought you might feel this way, Mr. Heart," Sonja said. "I have a recommendation that I hope you'll consider."

"What?"

"When was the last time you went to a Heart store?" she asked.

Cole got up and paced the area between the table and his large desk. "I'm always in the stores. What's your point?"

Sonja sat back and crossed her legs. "Yes, you're in the stores as the chief executive officer of the company. But have you been in one as a customer lately? I suggest you go to a couple of Heart Department Stores and see for yourself."

"I'd be recognized."

"Get in disguise. It's not that difficult."

"That's ridiculous."

Sonja shut down the computer. "Mr. Heart, you hired my firm to give you a snapshot of your world. The film's been developed, and you don't like the photographs. I'm simply suggesting that you go shoot your own film, and see how your pictures fare before you discredit the very thing you requested from me. If you thought everything was rosy you never would have contacted The Pride Group."

Chapter 2

She was right, and he knew it. That's what pissed Cole off so much. He'd already suspected every negative thing she said. Numbers didn't lie, no matter how desperately he wanted a rosier economic outlook for the company. It hurt to have an outsider waltz in and nail him in the space of a month on the very shortcomings he suspected to be the cause of depleted resources and profit from his department stores.

Cole wanted to believe it wasn't true.

He also wanted to believe that a woman as delicate as Sonja Pride would buckle when faced with his wrath. She didn't. Reluctantly, Cole admitted to himself that he liked that. A lot. Just as he admired the fact that she'd been early, even though she'd caught him not completely dressed for their appointment.

No one had caught Cole Heart unprepared for years—twenty-five to be exact—not since he was ten-years-old, and his cousin underbid him for the lease of a lemonade stand.

As Sonja sat there waiting, he continued pacing the room, mulling over her recommendation and wondering why he'd noticed the way she smiled at Lance.

Suddenly, he turned to face her.

"What kind of disguise?" he asked.

"That's up to you," she said, cool as you please.

"How did your people dress?"

"It depended on their tasks. My independent shoppers went in as if they were ordinary customers. The permanent staff acted according to the guidelines you set in the initial memo you sent. Sometimes professional, sometimes scruffy, sometimes confused, at other times demanding."

"In other words, just like real customers?" Lance asked.

Sonja smiled at him. "Exactly."

Out of nowhere, a stab of jealousy attacked Cole, and the beginning of a bad mood cropped up.

"Lance, don't you have something else to do?"

"Huh?" Surprised at the tone and obviously wondering what he'd done this time, Lance looked up.

"I'd like that youth department analysis on my desk in an hour."

Lance glanced between the stony Cole and an unfazed Sonja. "Uh, okay, Cole. I'll get right on it."

He excused himself. Then, with a farewell to Sonja and one last longing look at the laptop, Lance slipped out of the office.

With the pup gone, Cole leaned two hands on the table where Sonja still sat. It was time to get to the truth.

"Why are my employees stealing from me?"

He stared at her, willing the gospel from her lips. Unflinching, Sonja met his unspoken challenge.

"Because you let them."

Cole stood up and folded his arms. Staring down his patrician nose, he studied her. Her skin was suntanned honey, a smooth light brown, darker than his own. Her wide eyes would speak volumes, given the right circumstance. He wondered what they looked like smoky with passion. Sonja Pride's full mouth begged notice. Cole decided it was best to concentrate on something else.

He would have expected her to wear red, the corporate power color. But Sonja Pride wore white. Clean, honest, virginal white. Her formfitting suit, one he recognized as *not* purchased at a Heart store, had been altered to compliment her figure.

"Where do you shop, Ms. Pride?"

Surprised, she blinked. Cole kept a small smile to himself.

"I don't see the relevance of that question," she said.

He nodded toward her suit. "That's not from a Heart Department Store."

"No, it's not," she said, meeting his challenging look.

The staring game continued. Cole conceded that he'd met a worthy adversary. His alpha responded to her omega on levels he hadn't bothered to deal with in a while. Not at all liking the flow of his thought, Cole decided to end the meeting.

"Be back here in a week," he said. "Make the appointment with Mason," he added over his shoulder as he walked to his desk chair.

Sonja stood. "Why? The Pride Group's work is complete. We've done all you requested. Extra copies of the findings are available for your board members."

She reached for the cord to unplug it from the table socket.

"*If,*" he said, stressing the word, "if your field report is accurate, your work, Ms. Pride, is just beginning."

With that he sat in his chair and punched up a program on his PC .

Sonja was dismissed.

* * *

Later, Sonja still seethed. The audacity of that arrogant son of a . . .

Take a deep breath, she coached herself on the drive back to her office. *You've come too far to let ego get in the way now.*

She'd taken her sweet time leaving his office. From his computer he'd scowled at her twice before she was packed up and ready to go.

When she stood in front of his desk and extended her hand to say "Good-bye", he looked as if he'd rather suck snake venom than touch her.

So be it, you self-righteous jerk. Your day is coming, my brother. Your day is coming, she silently fumed.

On the rest of the drive to her office, Sonja kept her mind occupied with the ways she'd celebrate Cole Heart's downfall.

The tile floors were dirty. The courtesy shopping bag racks were empty. Barely ten steps in the door, Cole counted three burned out lightbulbs in a display featuring vintage era clothing.

Making his way to the nearest cash register, he stood aside while the clerk waited on a customer.

The clerk smiled at Cole, acknowledging the new

customer's presence, then turned his attention back to his current customer.

"We don't seem to have that in stock, Ma'am. What I can do is put it on back order for you. It should take three to seven days to come in. If you'll complete this form, I'll call you when it arrives."

The customer wrote her name and number on the form, then the clerk handed her a piece of paper. "I do apologize for the delay this is causing you. That's a coupon for twenty percent off any item in the store. You can use it today or save it for when the jacket comes in."

Cole watched the woman's face light up as she accepted the coupon. "Twenty percent, huh? Make my own sale. That's nice. Thank you."

"You're more than welcome."

Like an approving coach, Cole nodded. Peering through the thick glass spectacles he'd donned as part of his disguise, he made note of the employee's name: Gene. He'd done everything right. Where were Sonja Pride's people when this clerk was working? This was more like the store and the employees he knew. Sonja Pride was full of it.

As the customer moved on, Cole stepped up.

"How may I help you today, sir?" the clerk asked.

"I'm looking for a present for my, uh, wife," Cole said stroking the thick, fake mustache and beard he'd found to help shield his identity.

"Was there anything you had in mind? This is the

men's department, but I can make several suggestions. Quite a few ladies like to wear mens' pajama tops."

Cole shook his head and smoothed the itchy beard. "No. I'm looking for female things. You know, something womany. Stuff that looks good and smells good."

The clerk smiled. "Let me show you how to get to our fragrance department. Right next to it you'll find women's accessories."

Gene stepped around his cash register area and walked several feet with Cole. He paused when he came to the threshold of his department. "If you stay right along this walkway you'll run into fragrances. You'll know you're in the right place when you see a display of candles. And it'll smell good."

"Well, thank you. That's mighty helpful."

"You're quite welcome. Have a pleasant Heart experience."

Cole smiled as he made his way past a display of men's hats and a bank of monitors featuring the latest mens' accessories from international designers.

Gene had provided a textbook service encounter. His customer left without what she came in the store for, but with the inconvenience coupon in hand she would probably find several things that caught her eye before she actually left the store. And she'd tell her friends about her good experience at Heart.

The clerk had just earned himself a Heart token,

doled out for exemplary customer service, or doing something right. Cole remembered the first one he'd earned from his grandfather. To this day employees who earned a Heart token could redeem it for twenty-five dollars worth of store merchandise, twenty-five dollars in cash, or an hour of personal time.

Cole loved being in retail, and he loved his stores. He liked the texture of the merchandise, the colors, the music piped in on hidden speakers, the hearts embedded in the tile floors. He liked the effort put into, and the effect of, creative displays that attracted the eye. He liked making customers happy.

As he approached and paused at a clearance table of boys' shirts, Cole automatically reached out to straighten and refold the piles of merchandise. He peeked around. No one was watching, and there wasn't a clerk in sight. He made quick work of organizing the shirts. Then he meandered into the boys' department. Several customers milled about. One stood at a cash register looking around for some help. Cole recognized the signs of impatient agitation in the woman.

Where the hell were the clerks?

If he waited on the customer his cover would be blown. If he didn't, she'd leave Heart unsatisfied.

Cole figured he could mitigate the damage.

He grabbed a shirt from a rack and sidled up to her. "Hi," he said.

The woman glanced over at him. "I tell you, you can never find any help in this place," she groused.

"Ever?" Cole asked.

The woman frowned at him.

"There's a guy over there," he said, pointing to the nearby men's department. "He was real helpful. You can check out with him. Gene was his name."

"Thanks," the woman mumbled.

She scooped up about forty dollars' worth of boys' underwear and T-shirts and headed in the direction Cole had suggested.

Still no clerk. And another customer was headed to the register.

Cole bit back a frustrated curse and looked around the department. A flash of orange near the fitting room caught his eye. With the shirt in hand, he marched in that direction.

"Girl, I don't know what I'm gonna wear. When he asked me out, I was just all to pieces."

"Why don't you get something to go with that gold—"

Cole interrupted the conversation. "Excuse me, do either of you work here?"

A woman in green slacks and an orange floral top turned around. "Something I can help you with?"

He took in her name: LaKeisha. "There are people out there waiting to be waited on. And one woman just left because no one was around to help her. You need to be minding your department and customers instead of standing around gossiping."

"Excuse me." Her words weren't a polite good-bye to her co-worker.

Cole's eyes narrowed. Then he remembered his role. He held up the shirt. "Do you have this in a size eight?"

LaKeisha rolled her eyes at her friend, then went to take care of her register. The other one, Gretta, took the shirt from Cole.

"I'll check on that for you," she said.

He followed her toward the rack of Oxford cloth shirts. "How long have you worked here?" he asked.

"About a year," Gretta replied.

"What about your friend?"

The clerk searched through the shirts. "LaKeisha? She's new here. Just a couple of months." She pulled two shirts from the rack, one white and one blue. "Would you like either of these? They're both size eight."

Cole handed her the shirt he held. "I'll take the white one."

"Anything else for you today, sir?"

"Nothing else," he said, then followed her to the two-register station.

"No, we all out of that," he heard LaKeisha say.

Cole cringed at her abuse of the language and stepped to his left so he could better watch her encounter with the customer.

"Well, is there a substitute?" the customer asked. "It's in this week's sale paper."

"We sold out. Sorry."

Offer an alternative, Cole screamed to himself. But LaKeisha just stood there.

Cole's scowl grew deeper. Gretta must have seen his consternation. "Is there something else I can find for you?"

"I'll look around for a minute. Your co-worker sounds like she needs some help. You seem to be out of what that lady came in for," he said.

And your friend is going to be out of a job in the morning if she doesn't get her act together, he added to himself.

As if she had read his thoughts, Gretta quickly moved to offer LaKeisha some help.

A few minutes later, he approached the register with the white shirt and a couple of items he'd picked up for show.

He watched as LaKeisha policed the department and Gretta waited on a customer. Gretta closed the sale the way she should have. "Thank you for your patience," she said. "Have a good rest of the day."

Cole was smiling by the time he left the boys' department. LaKeisha's longterm employment prospects were dim. As for Gretta, she hadn't earned a Heart token, but she'd redeemed herself in his eyes. The contented look left his face when he saw the messy state of the candle and stationery area and got a look at the clerk minding the area.

"What *is* this, Halloween?" he mumbled.

The woman's jet black, straight hair matched her heavy, black eye makeup, which matched her black lipstick, and her hideously long, black fingernails. A long black skirt and a black see-right-through-to-a-black-bra chiffon blouse completed the ghoulish and totally inappropriate get-up.

Cole's faint hope that the woman was a customer and not one of his employees flickered and died the instant she flipped her hair over her shoulder. The red and white Heart Department Store name badge was the only relief of color on the woman, and the one thing Cole didn't want to see.

He felt, actually felt, his blood pressure rising as he watched her.

Cole wanted to snatch the badge that associated her with his store. In that costume, she'd scare all the customers away.

Saying adults who worked in retail could be trusted to come to work in appropriate business attire, Cole had twice vetoed a proposal establishing a dress code for employees. Now he saw the merit in the plan. Some people had no judgment at all.

She looked as if she'd bite the head off of anyone who dared approach. Cole dared.

"Are you going to a costume party?"

The woman didn't crack a smile. "I believe in expressing the individuality of my awareness with the elements. I mourn the destruction of our planet."

"Do you work here?"

She blinked. "I am currently employed by this capitalistic stronghold."

Capitalistic stronghold? "Not for long," he snapped back. Why the hell was she working in a department store? He peered through his glasses at her name: Millicent.

"Is there an overpriced piece of shoddily-made merchandise produced by underage, underpaid, southeast Asian workers that I can find for you?" she asked.

In an instant, Cole's anger became a scalding fury. His lips thinned to a line so sharp they could cut paper.

"What the—"

A single tenuous thread of rationality and control was the only thing that kept Cole from bodily ejecting the woman from his store. How dare she stand there and spout that trash to a customer?

Without another word Cole stormed away. That Millicent creature wouldn't be on his payroll by the end of the day.

He paused near the escalators and pulled his tiny cell phone from a pocket. Mason was on the line immediately.

"I'm at the Virginia Beach store. There's a Millicent in stationery and gifts. I want her terminated by 5 P.M. Get her supervisor and his or her supervisor in my office immediately. Put all three files on my desk."

He slammed the phone shut and stared unseeing at the colorful displays near him and the people streaming by.

So furious he could hardly think straight, Cole speed-dialed his assistant again.

"Yes, sir?"

"And get Sonja Pride in my office first thing in the morning."

Chapter 3

It took Cole a long time to calm down. The forty-minute drive to the corporate office in Hampton would have helped if he hadn't been on the telephone yelling at the Virginia Beach store manager.

Now, hours later, he still couldn't believe that a Heart employee had said the things that woman said to him. How many customers had she assaulted that way? How much damage had she done?

In the poolroom of his Williamsburg house that overlooked the gated community's world-class golf course, Cole swam laps, trying to get his still seething temper under control.

To the man's credit, the store manager had taken total responsibility. The immediate supervisor said Millicent was about to be fired, anyway. Reviewing the conversation as he swam didn't help his state of mind.

No wonder Heart stores had fared so dismally with Sonja Pride's mystery shoppers. If the company was losing money, it was because the freaking employees were sabotaging him.

Cole gave up the swimming. At this rate, he'd drown. Hauling himself from the water, he reached for a towel.

"That's some mighty aggressive swimming, cousin."

Cole had thought the day couldn't get any worse.

"Who let you in?" he asked his cousin Mallory.

"I came with your mother."

Worse took a downhill turn.

Cole's head started pounding. "What do you want?"

"Is that any way to treat family? I heard you were on the warpath today."

Good news always spread quickly in the Heart family.

"And your point?" he asked as he dried his legs.

"Cole, darling. There you are," Virginia Heart called. "I have someone I want you to meet."

Her heels clicked on the tile of the poolside area.

If he'd told her once, he'd told her a thousand times that high heels and wet tile didn't go together.

"Mother, please be careful."

"Oh, you're such a worrywart. I've been walking on my own feet for sixty-two years. I'm perfectly fine. I'd like you to meet Andrea Delhaven. She's Senator Delhaven's daughter."

His mother stepped aside and presented a cover-model beautiful woman. Yet another one. Cole sighed. Virginia beamed as the introduction was made.

Cole wanted to be polite. He just didn't have it in him right then. He shook the woman's hand. "Pleased to meet you. Excuse me."

He brushed past all three astonished women and snatched up the cell phone he'd left on a chaise. He'd find no peace in his own house tonight, not with his mother and cousin underfoot.

In the dressing room, Cole showered and quickly dressed. Then, without a word to anyone, he slipped out a side door and made his way to the four-car garage, a bottle of Mylanta in his hand.

Taking a swig of the antacid, Cole steered his Town Car toward the tourist area of historic Williamsburg. A night in a hotel room would be preferable to time spent in his own house with his matchmaking mother and his calculating cousin.

* * *

Sonja refused to be summoned like one of Cole Heart's flunkies. The entire Heart family had an over-inflated sense of importance. Sure, they were wealthy, but so was Sonja. Sure, the Hearts were influential in the area, even the state, but by no measure was Heart Federated her most important client.

As a matter of fact, for what the company requested and what they were paying, the Heart account had already gotten more than it merited—a whole lot more, as Sonja's vice-president of operations kept telling her. But this job was personal, and Sonja wanted to dot all the I's and cross all the T's—twice.

If Cole Heart wanted to meet with her, he could set an appointment like anyone else. And Sonja had told the ever-efficient Mason just that.

Sonja smiled. He'd probably taken her up on her idea about being a customer in his stores. "And I'll just bet you got a taste of your own Heart experience. I hope it gave you heartburn."

Instead of walking into Cole Heart's office at eight o'clock the next morning, Sonja headed to the weekly meeting of her executive committee.

The operations vice-president started his report with Sonja's trademark saying. "I've got good news, and bad news."

Sonja reached for her coffee and took a sip. "Bad news first."

Brian Jackson smiled. "Well, it's bad for us, but good for a company in Minneapolis."

Sonja sat up fast and darted an anxious gaze around the table at her three most trusted employees, people she was proud to call friends as well as colleagues.

"Calm down, Sonja," Brian said. "It's not one of us."

Good-natured chuckles around the room eased her. Being preoccupied with Cole Heart had her on edge these days.

"So, what's the news?" she asked Brian.

"Micah Adams is leaving. He's taken a position as manager of product content for an on-line investment firm."

Sonja nodded. "Good for him. Party and send-off?"

Renita, the employee relations vice-president, glanced at her planner. "Two weeks from today. Five o'clock."

Sonja made a notation in her electronic planner, then looked at the group. "And the good news would be?"

Brian glanced around, then smiled broadly as he plopped a thick sheaf of papers in the middle of the table.

"The Robinson account. It's ours. Signed, sealed, and delivered."

Whoops of joy and high fives went around the room. Sonja's smile was the biggest of all.

"Excellent! That's excellent. Congratulations, Brian and Renita. Good work all around."

Brian beamed.

Sonja rose and addressed the group. "For the last three months, we've been in neck and neck competition to land this account. As you know, Robinson's convenience stores are on practically every other block in the country." She reached for and held up the contract. "This revenue is going to be staggering."

Cheers around the room filled Sonja's ears, and she loved it. Her company made its money by evaluating the business climate for companies, as she had for Cole Heart. Through a network of about two hundred professional evaluaters known as mystery shoppers and a full-time work force of thirty-five, The Pride Group offered assessment, evaluation, market comparison, and for companies requesting the additional services, diversity and customer service training.

Steady growth and careful planning kept the eight-year-old firm on solid financial ground. Sonja believed in rewarding her people for good work. News of landing the Robinson account meant the fat cash bonuses Sonja had promised the executive group if they pulled it off would be a reality. She wanted to take care of the rest of her people, too.

"Can we afford to give everyone a paid personal

day?" she asked Janice, who oversaw the finance division.

"Everyone? Like all the full-timers?"

"And the interns," Sonja said.

Janice nodded. "Just so you know, the cash option would be cheaper and less of an administrative headache."

Feeling generous, Sonja waved a hand. "Let each person choose." And it was done. Everyone around the table grinned.

The rest of the long meeting went by with reports from the executive group members about their respective areas. Brian's report about staff operations took the biggest chunk of time as he gave a summary of active accounts, each known as a shop. The group discussed the shops on an as needed basis. Listening attentively, Sonja weighed in with questions or kudos where warranted.

"There's the unfinished business of the Heart Federated Stores," Brian said.

"I'll close that one out," Sonja piped up before anyone could say anything.

Renita glanced at Brian, who shrugged.

"I met with the CEO yesterday and presented the findings. He wasn't pleased." Sonja said. She didn't even try to keep the smile from her voice.

Renita and Brian exchanged glances again.

"Anything else?" Sonja asked the group.

When no one offered anything else, Sonja called the meeting a wrap.

Half an hour later, she stood in her office overlooking the Hampton River. The boats docked at the marinas and the serene view of Hampton University should have calmed her, but they didn't. Her nerves were frayed.

A quick four tap, followed by a two count rat-a-tat on her door, let her know Brian stood on the other side.

"Come on in," she called over her shoulder.

The soft whoosh of air let her know he'd entered.

"Congratulations," she told him.

"Thank you."

"I knew you could do it," she said, finally turning to him.

"You gave me the shot."

Itching to prove something to himself and to her, Brian had practically begged to handle the negotiations on the Robinson deal. Sonja knew that if she hadn't been distracted by Cole Heart, she'd never have given Brian the leeway to work as he did. The Pride Group was small enough, and Sonja cared enough to be in on every major deal. As it turned out, Brian's involvement was probably for the best. He'd given the account one hundred percent. Being honest with herself, Sonja knew the Robinson people wouldn't have gotten her best work.

"Headed to Jamaica or Bermuda with your bonus?" she asked.

"Only if you'll agree to join me."

Sonja sighed and turned back to gaze out the window. "Brian, let's not go there now, okay?"

She took his silence for acquiescence.

"Do you want to tell me what's going on with this Heart Federated shop?"

"No."

Brian's eyebrows rose. "Okay," he said slowly. "You do know that we've expended considerable resources on a job with marginal return. They didn't even request half the stuff we've done. Are we going to bill them for all of the time and effort?"

"No."

Sonja stood at the window behind her desk, staring at the river and at traffic crossing the bridge leading to downtown Hampton.

Brian sighed. He came around the desk and stood next to her.

"What's personal about this Heart account? You're not telling me something."

"It's nothing, Brian. I'm just working, already. Okay? That's what we do here."

"It's a dead end account," he said. "Yeah, they have eight stores, but they don't want anything but this. You said so yourself. Since when do you get so involved in a little pissant account like that?"

"Since now, all right? I'm handling it."

She turned toward him and caught the hurt expression on his face before he masked his feelings. In recent months it had become increasingly difficult for Brian to separate his business acumen from his attraction to Sonja. Sonja knew the blame for their current personal situation fell at her feet, but right now she had so many tugs on her time and her thoughts that she couldn't deal with this part of Brian.

"It's me, honey. You know you can talk to me about anything."

"Don't call me 'honey,' Brian. I've told you that before."

He let out an exasperated sigh, then rubbed his eyes.

"I just want to help you," he said. "You've been tense and irritable, not yourself for the last few weeks. I'm not the only person who's noticed or who's worried about you."

"I'm fine. I'm fine. I'm *fine.*" Sonja gritted her teeth in an exaggerated smile. "See?"

"Yeah, I see. That's what worries me."

After Brian left, Sonja sat at her desk staring at her door. She wondered just what others saw in her these last few weeks.

She knew she wasn't fine, as she claimed—far from it.

Sonja Pride, businesswoman, entrepreneur, survivor, had become obsessed. The only way to get rid of the obsession was to eliminate the problem.

Her gaze fell to the telephone. She reached for the receiver and started dialing the number of Heart's corporate office. The fact that she knew the number from memory made her pause. A chill ran through her, and she rubbed her arms.

Before the first ring, Sonja replaced the receiver.

She was where she was today, doing what she did, because of Cole Heart and his family. None of them knew that, of course. They wouldn't have cared if they *had* known. That's just how they were.

Her animosity toward the Hearts had started a long time ago. . . .

Sonja had enough money to buy her mom the pretty, silk scarf. She'd saved almost a dollar a week by not buying milk at lunch. Even though her mother never said anything, Sonja knew they were poor. She'd learned not to ask for the expensive jeans and sneakers that the other girls wore to school. Her clothes were always clean and pressed, even if they weren't quite in style.

Once she'd seen her mom crying. It frightened Sonja. Her mother was strong, and everything was safe in her arms. But when Sonja asked about the wet tracks on her face, her mom simply wiped at her eyes and held her arms open for Sonja. The big hug made everything better.

She smoothed one small finger down the soft fabric.

This scarf would go perfectly with the blue dress mom wore to church sometimes, but so would the red one.

"May I help you, little girl?"

Sonja smiled up at the clerk. "I'm thinking about this scarf. It's for my mom."

The Heart Department Store clerk smiled at her, then looked at the price tag. "It's pretty, isn't it?"

Sonja bobbed her head accordingly.

"Do you have enough money?"

"Yes, ma'am. I've been saving up. Now I just have to decide which one."

The clerk smiled at her again, and Sonja knew she'd made a friend.

"Well, my name is Marie. I'll be right over there. Call for me when you decide, okay?"

"Yes, Miss Marie."

With another smile for her, the clerk headed to a display of Easter hats.

Sonja's consideration of the scarves continued for several minutes. Her mind made up on the blue one, she glanced around for Miss Marie, then reached for the delicate material.

"Just hold it right there, you."

Sonja froze and gripped the scarf in a suddenly tight hand.

When she turned around, she saw that the shrill voice belonged to an older lady with wrinkles around her mouth and pin curls so sharp you could cut a finger on them.

"I've been watching you. Did you think you were going to steal that today?"

Sonja's eyes widened, and she released her hold on the scarf. "No, ma'am. I'm going to buy—"

But the woman cut her off. "Security alert. Security alert."

Sonja's frightened gaze darted around the area. Several people had turned to stare. "No, you don't understand. Miss Marie—"

A burly security guard appeared out of thin air and grabbed Sonja's arm. "All right, little lady. This way with you."

"But I didn't do anything."

"Yeah, yeah. That's what they all say," the guard said as he escorted her away.

But not before Sonja heard the wrinkled saleslady tell another patron, "Just like their kind. Trashy. Always looking for a way to take something that doesn't belong to them."

Squirming in the security guard's grip, Sonja turned to get another look at her accuser. The woman smiled and a chill ran through Sonja. Again she looked for the nice Miss Marie, but didn't see her.

The guard led her to a small office in the back of the store, where she was questioned for half an hour. Then her mother was summoned from work. The surprise was ruined, and her mom had lost wages because she had to come get Sonja. . . .

The shrill ring of the telephone startled Sonja.

Blinking several times, she glanced around. She wasn't in a Heart Department Store. She wasn't eight-years-old. She didn't stand erroneously accused of trying to steal.

She was thirty-three years old, and about to pay the Hearts back for that first of many indignities.

A Note to Readers from Felicia Mason

Sometimes the ideas that come in the heat of the moment are such good ones. Then comes the follow-up. Mallory Heart's story is one of those follow-ups.

Introduced in FOOLISH HEART as the evil woman whose sole purpose in life seemed to be to thwart any business move made by her cousin Coleman Heart, Mallory was tough and no-nonsense, a heroine in the rough. Cole and Mallory had been rivals all of their lives. But Mallory's anger, so much a living thing, kept me wondering about her and whether she could, indeed, become a true heroine.

"Why is this woman so mean?" That's the question that kept nagging at me about her. And then, in that way that characters do, she told me and I began to write. Mallory needed that thing that we all need deep down: to be loved for who we are, not what we are.

My wish is that you have—or that you'll eventually find—the love of your life, and that you'll be loved for who you are, warts and blemishes along with all the terrific stuff that make you the unique person you are.

May joy and peace fill your heart,
Felicia Mason

To access Felicia Mason's Web site, go to:
www.geocities.com/Paris/Gallery/9250/

ABOUT THE AUTHOR

Felicia Mason is an award-winning journalist and author. Her novels include *Rhapsody, Seduction, For the Love of You, Body and Soul,* and *Foolish Heart.* In 1997, *For the Love of You* was named one of *Glamour* magazine readers' all-time "Favorite Love Stories."

Mason is a two-time winner of the Best-Selling Multicultural Title Award from Waldenbooks. Her work has also received a Reviewer's Choice Award from *Romantic Times,* and the Best Contemporary Ethnic Novel Award from *Affaire de Coeur.*

She lives in Virginia.

SIZZLING ROMANCE FROM *FELICIA MASON*

For the Love of You **0-7860-0071-6** **$4.99**US/**$6.50**CAN
Years of hard work had finally provided a secure life for Kendra Edwards but when she meets high-powered attorney Malcolm Hightower, he arouses desires that she swore she would never let herself feel again . . .

Body and Soul **0-7860-0160-7** **$4.99**US/**$6.50**CAN
Toinette Blue's world is her children and her successful career as the director of a woman's counseling group . . . until devastatingly handsome, much younger attorney Robinson Mayview rekindles the flames of a passion that both excites and frightens her . . .

Seduction **0-7860-0297-2** **$4.99**US/**$6.50**CAN
C.J. Mayview goes to North Carolina for peace of mind and to start anew. But secrets unravel when U.S. Marshal Wes Donovan makes it his business to discover all there is to know about the beautiful journalist . . .

Foolish Heart **0-7860-0593-9** **$4.99**US/**$6.50**CAN
Intent on saving his business, Coleman Heart III turns to beautiful consultant Sonja Pride. But Sonja has a debt to pay the Heart family, and she is determined to seek revenge until she finds out that Coleman is a caring, honorable man to whom she just might be able to give her heart.

USE COUPON ON NEXT PAGE TO ORDER THESE BOOKS